Return items to **any** Swindon library by closing
time on or before the date stamped. Only books
and Audio Books can be renewed - phone your
library or visit our website. *PAR*
www.swindon.gov.uk/libraries

Park Library
12 15
Tel: 01793 463501

1 SEP 2018

ACq>EVE
31.12.15

PARDINTH
23/6

01. FEB 16.

BROAD, E

THOMAS

Even Swindon Library
Jennings Street
SN2 2BG
01793 934019

08 18

Copying recordings is illegal. All recorded items
are hired entirely at hirer's own risk

Swindon
BOROUGH COUNCIL

and rubbed

warning

Lean dro.

D1180961

The Ravensdale Scandals

Scandal is this family's middle name!

With notoriously famous parents, the Ravensdale
children grew up in the limelight. But *nothing* could
have prepared them for this latest scandal…
the revelation of a Ravensdale love-child!

London's most eligible siblings find themselves
in the eye of their own paparazzi storm.
They're determined to fight back—
they just never factored in falling in love too…!

Find out what happens in
Julius Ravensdale's story
Ravensdale's Defiant Captive
December 2015

Miranda Ravensdale's story
Awakening the Ravensdale Heiress
January 2016

And watch for Jake and Katherine's
Ravensdale Scandals…coming soon!

AWAKENING THE RAVENSDALE HEIRESS

BY
MELANIE MILBURNE

Published in Great Britain 2016
by Mills & Boon, an imprint of Harlequin (UK) Limited,
Eton House, 18-24 Paradise Road, Richmond, Surrey, TW9 1SR

ISBN: 978-0-263-91581-5

An avid romance reader, **Melanie Milburne** loves writing the books that gave her so much joy as she was busy getting married to her own hero and raising a family. Now a *USA TODAY* bestselling author, she has won several awards—including The Australian Readers' Association most popular category/ series romance in 2008 and the prestigious Romance Writers of Australia R*BY award in 2011.

She loves to hear from readers!

MelanieMilburne.com.au
Facebook.com/Melanie.Milburne
Twitter @MelanieMilburn1

Books by Melanie Milburne

Mills & Boon Modern Romance

At No Man's Command
His Final Bargain
Uncovering the Silveri Secret
Surrendering All But Her Heart
His Poor Little Rich Girl

The Ravensdale Scandals

Ravensdale's Defiant Captive

The Chatsfield

Chatsfield's Ultimate Acquisition

The Playboys of Argentina

The Valquez Bride
The Valquez Seduction

Those Scandalous Caffarellis

Never Say No to a Caffarelli
Never Underestimate a Caffarelli
Never Gamble with a Caffarelli

The Outrageous Sisters

Deserving of His Diamonds?
Enemies at the Altar

Visit the Author Profile page at
millsandboon.co.uk for more titles.

To Holly Marks.
Thank you for being such a wonderful fan.
Your lovely comments on Facebook
have lifted me so many times.
This one is for you with much love and appreciation.
xxxx

CHAPTER ONE

MIRANDA WOULDN'T HAVE seen him if she hadn't been hiding from the paparazzi. Not that a fake potted plant was a great hiding place or anything, she thought. She peeped through the branches of the ornamental ficus to see Leandro Allegretti crossing the busy street outside the coffee shop she was sheltering in. He didn't seem aware of the fact it was spitting with rain or that the intersection was clotted with traffic and bustling with pedestrians. It was as if a transparent cube was around him. He was impervious to the chatter and clatter outside.

She would have recognised him anywhere. He had a regal, untouchable air about him that made him stand out in a crowd. Even the way he was dressed set him apart—not that there weren't other suited men in the crowd, but the way he wore the sharply tailored charcoal-grey suit teamed with a snowy white shirt and a black-and-silver striped tie somehow made him look different. More civilised. More dignified.

Or maybe it was because of his signature frown.

Had she ever seen him without that frown? Miranda wondered. Her older twin brothers, Julius and Jake, had been boarding school buddies with Leandro. He had spent occasional weekends or school holidays and even university breaks at the Ravensdale family home, Ravensdene, in Buckinghamshire. Being a decade younger, she'd spent most of her childhood being a little intimidated by Leandro's taciturn presence. He was the epitome of the strong, silent type—a man of few words and even fewer facial expressions. She couldn't read his expression at the best of times. It was hard to tell if he was frowning in disapproval or simply in deep concentration.

He came into the coffee shop and Miranda watched as every female head turned his way. His French-Italian heritage had served him well in the looks department. Imposingly tall with jet-black hair, olive skin and brown eyes three or four shades darker than hers.

But if Leandro was aware of his impact on the female gaze he gave no sign of it. It was one of the things she secretly most liked about him. He didn't trade on his appearance. He seemed largely unaware of how knee-wobblingly gorgeous he looked. It was as if it was irrelevant to him. Unlike her brother Jake, who knew he was considered arm candy and exploited it for all he could.

Leandro stood at the counter and ordered a long black coffee to take away from the young, blushing attendant, and then politely stood back to wait for it, taking out his phone to check his messages or emails.

Miranda covertly studied his tall, athletic figure with its strongly corded muscles honed from long hours of endurance exercise. The broad shoulders, the strong back, the lean hips, taut buttocks and the long legs. She had seen him many a time down at Ravensdene, a solitary figure running across the fields of the estate in all sorts of weather, or swimming endless laps of the pool in summer.

Leandro took to exercise with an intense, single-minded concentration that made her wonder if he was doing it for the health benefits or for some other reason known only to himself. But, whatever reason it was that motivated him, it clearly worked to his benefit. He had the sort of body to stop female hearts. She couldn't stop looking at him, drinking in the male perfection of his frame, her mind traitorously wondering how delicious he would look in a tangle of sheets after marathon sex. Did he have a current lover? Miranda hadn't heard much about his love life lately, but she'd heard his father had died a couple of months ago. She assumed he'd been keeping a low profile since.

The young attendant handed Leandro his coffee and as he turned to leave his eyes met Miranda's through the craggy branches of the pot plant. She saw the flash of recognition go through his gaze but he didn't smile in welcome. His lips didn't even twitch upwards. But then, she couldn't remember ever seeing him smile. Or, at least, not at her. The closest he came to it was a sort of twist of his lips that could easily be mistaken for cynicism rather than amusement.

'Miranda?' he said.

She lifted her hand in a little fingertip wave, trying

not to draw too much attention to herself in case anyone lurking nearby with a smart phone recognised her. 'Hi.'

He came over to her table screened behind the pot plant. She had to crane her neck to meet his frowning gaze. She always felt like a pixie standing in front of a giant when she was around him. He was an inch shorter than her six-foot-four brothers but for some reason he'd always seemed taller.

'Are the press still hassling you?' he asked, still frowning.

Of course, Leandro had heard about her father's scandal, Miranda thought. It was the topic on everyone's lips. It was splashed over every newsfeed or online blog. Could it get any more embarrassing? Was there anyone in London—*the entire world*—who didn't know her father had sired a love child twenty-three years ago? As London theatre royalty, her parents were known for drawing attention to themselves. But this scandal of her father's was the biggest and most mortifying so far. Miranda's mother, Elisabetta Albertini, had cancelled her season on Broadway and was threatening divorce. Her father, Richard Ravensdale, was trying to get his love child into the bosom of the family but so far with zero success. Apparently Katherine Winwood had failed to be charmed by her long-lost biological father and was doing everything she could to avoid him and her half-siblings.

Which was fine by Miranda. Just fine, especially since Kat was so beautiful that everyone was calling Miranda 'the ugly sister'. *Argh!*

'Just a little,' Miranda said with a pained smile. 'But

enough about all that. I'm so sorry about your father. I didn't know about him passing otherwise I would've come to the funeral.'

'Thank you,' he said. 'But it was a private affair.'

'So, how are things with you?' she said. 'I heard you did some work for Julius in Argentina. Great news about his engagement, isn't it? I met his fiancée Holly last night. She's lovely.' Miranda always found it difficult to make conversation with Leandro. He wasn't the small talk type. When she was around him she had a tendency to babble or ramble to fill any silence with the first thing that came into her head. She knew it made her seem a little vacuous, but he was so tight-lipped, what else was she to do? She felt like a tennis-ball machine loping balls at him but without him returning any.

Fortunately this time he did.

'Yes,' he said. 'Great news.'

'It was a big surprise, wasn't it?' Miranda said. 'I didn't even know he was dating anyone. I can't believe my big brother is getting married. Seriously, Julius is such a dark horse, he's practically invisible. But Holly is absolutely perfect for him. I'm so happy for them. Jasmine Connolly is going to design the wedding dress. We're both going to be bridesmaids, as Holly doesn't have any sisters or close friends. I don't know why she doesn't have loads of friends because she's such a sweetheart. Jaz thinks so too. You remember Jaz, don't you? The gardener's daughter who grew up with me at Ravensdene? We went to school together. She's got her own bridal shop now and—'

'Can I ask a favour?'

Miranda blinked. A favour? What sort of favour? What was he going to say? *Shut up? Stop gabbling like a fool? Stop blushing like a gauche twelve-year-old schoolgirl?* 'Sure.'

His deep brown gaze was centred on hers, his dark brows still knitted together. 'Will you do a job for me?'

Her heart gave a funny little skip. 'Wh-what sort of job?' Stuttering was another thing she did when she was around him. What was it about this man that turned her into a gibbering idiot? It was ridiculous. She had known him *all* her life. He was like a brother to her…well, sort of. Leandro had always been on the fringe of her consciousness as the Ideal Man. Not that she ever allowed herself to indulge in such thoughts. Not fully. But they were there, like uninvited guests at a cocktail party, every now and again moving forward to sneak a canapé or a drink before melting back against the back wall of her mind.

'My father left me his art collection in his will,' Leandro said. 'I need someone to catalogue it before I can sell it; plus there are a couple of paintings that might need restoring. I'll pay you, of course.'

Miranda found it odd he hadn't told anyone his father had died until after the funeral was over. She wondered why he hadn't told her brothers, particularly Julius, who was the more serious and steady twin. Julius would have supported Leandro, gone to the funeral with him and stood by him if he'd needed back up.

She pictured Leandro standing alone at that funeral. Why had he gone solo? Funerals were horrible enough.

The final goodbye was always horrifically painful but to face it alone would be unimaginable. Even if he hadn't been close to his father there would still be grief for what he had missed out on, not to mention the heart-wrenching realisation it was now too late to fix it.

When her childhood sweetheart Mark Redbank had died of leukaemia, her family and his had surrounded her. Supported her. Comforted her. Even Leandro had turned up at the funeral—she remembered seeing his tall, silent dark-haired figure at the back of the church. It had touched her that he'd made the time when he'd hardly known Mark. He had only met him a handful of times.

Miranda had heard via her brothers that Leandro had a complicated back story. They hadn't told her much, only that his parents had divorced when he was eight years old and his mother had taken him to England, where he'd been promptly put into boarding school with Miranda's twin brothers after his mother had remarried and begun a new family. He had been a studious child, excelling both academically and on the sporting field. He had taken that hard work ethic into his career as a forensic accountant. 'I'm so sorry for your loss,' she said.

'Thank you.'

'Did your mother go to the funeral?' Miranda asked.

'No,' he said. 'They hadn't spoken since the divorce.'

Miranda wondered if his father's funeral would have brought back painful memories of his estranged relationship with him. No son wanted to be rejected by his father. But apparently Vittorio Allegretti hadn't wanted custody after the divorce. He had handed over Leandro as a small boy and only saw him on the rare occasion he'd been in London on business. She had heard via her brothers that eventually Leandro had stopped meeting his father because Vittorio had a tendency to drink to the point of abusing others and/or passing out. There had even been one occasion where the police had had to be called due to a bar-room scuffle Leandro's father had started. It didn't surprise her Leandro had kept his distance. With his quiet and reserved nature he wasn't the sort of man to draw unnecessary attention to himself.

But there was so much more she didn't know about him. She knew he was a forensic accountant—a brilliant one. He had his own consultancy in London and travelled all over the globe uncovering major fraud in the corporate and private sectors. He often worked with Jake with his business analysis company and he had recently helped Julius in exposing Holly's ghastly stepfather's underworld drug and money-laundering operations.

Leandro Allegretti was the go-to man for uncovering secrets and yet Miranda had always sensed he had one or two of his own.

'So this job…' she began. 'Where's the collection?'

'In Nice,' he said. 'My father ran an art and antiques business in the French Riviera. This is his private collection. He sold off everything else when he was first diagnosed with terminal cancer.'

'And you want to…to get rid of it?' Miranda asked,

frowning at the thought of him selling everything of his father's. In spite of their tricky relationship, didn't he want a memento? '*All* of it?'

The line of his mouth was flat. Hardened. Whitened. 'Yes,' he said. 'I have to pack up the villa and sell that too.'

'Why not use someone locally?' Miranda knew she was well regarded in her job as an art restorer even though she was at the early stages of her career. But she wouldn't be able to do much on site. Art restoration was more science now than art. Sophisticated techniques using x-rays, infrared technology and Raman spectroscopy meant most restoration work was done in the protective environment of an established gallery. Leandro could afford the best in the world. Why ask her?

'I thought you might like a chance to escape the hoo-hah here,' Leandro said. 'Can you take a couple of weeks' leave from the gallery?'

Miranda had already been thinking about getting out of London for some breathing space. It had been hell on wheels with her father's dirty linen being flapped in her face. She couldn't go anywhere without being assailed by press. Everyone wanted to know what she thought of her father's scandal. *Had she met her half-sister? Was she planning to? Were her parents divorcing for the second time?* It was relentless. Along with the press attention, she had also been subjected to her mother's bitter tirades about her father, and her father's insistence she make contact with her half-sister and play happy families.

Like that was going to happen.

This would be a perfect opportunity to escape. Besides, October on the Côte d'Azur would be preferable to the capricious weather London was currently dishing up. 'How soon do you want me?' she said, blushing when she realised her unintentional double entendre. 'I mean, I can probably get away from work by the end of next week. Is that okay?'

'Fine,' he said. 'I don't collect the keys to the villa until then anyway. I'll book your flight and email you the details. Do you have a preference for a hotel?'

'Where will you be staying?'

'At my father's villa.'

Miranda thought about the expense of staying at a hotel, not that Leandro couldn't afford it. He would put her in five-star accommodation if she asked for it. But staying in a hotel put her at risk of being found by the press. If she stayed with Leandro at his father's villa she could work on the collection without that looming threat.

Besides, it would be an opportunity to see a little of the man behind the perpetual frown.

'Is there room for me at your father's place?'

Leandro's frown deepened until two vertical lines formed between his bottomless brown eyes. 'You don't want to stay in a hotel?'

Miranda snagged her lip with her teeth, warm colour crawling further over her cheeks until her whole face felt on fire. 'I wouldn't want to intrude if you've got someone else staying...'

Who was his someone else?

Who was his latest lover? She knew he had them

from time to time. She had seen pictures of him at charity events. She had even met one or two over the years when he had brought a partner to one of the legendary parties her parents had put on at Ravensdene for New Year's Eve. Tall, impossibly beautiful, elegant, eloquent types who didn't blush and stumble over their words and make silly fools of themselves. He wasn't as out there as her playboy brother Jake. Leandro was more like Julius in that he liked to keep his private life out of the public domain.

'I haven't got anyone staying,' he said.

He hadn't got anyone staying? Or he hadn't got *anyone*?

And why was she even thinking about his love life? It wasn't as if she was interested in him. She was interested in no one. Not since Mark had died. She ignored attractive men. She quickly brushed off any men who flirted with her or tried to charm her. Not that Leandro was super-charming or anything. He was polite but distant. Aloof. And as for flirting…well, if he could learn to smile now and again it might help.

Miranda wasn't sure why she was pushing so hard for an invitation. Maybe it was because she had never spent any time with him without other people around. Maybe it was because he had recently lost his father and she wanted to know why he hadn't told anyone before the funeral. Maybe it was because she wanted to see where he had spent the first eight years of his life before he had moved to England. What had he been like as a child? Had he been playful and fun-loving, like most kids, or had he been as serious and inexpressive as he was now? 'So would it be okay to stay with you?' she said. 'I won't get in your way.'

He looked at her in that frowning manner he had. Deep thought or disapproval? She could never quite tell. 'There isn't a housekeeper there.'

'I can cook,' she said. 'And I can help you tidy things up before you sell the place. It'll be fun.'

A small silence ticked past.

Miranda got the feeling he was mulling it over. Weighing it up in his mind. Doing a risk assessment.

He finally drew in a breath and then slowly released it. 'Fine. I'll email you those flights.'

She rose from the table and began to shrug on her coat, tugging her hair free from the collar. 'Do you mind if I walk out with you? There was a pap crew tailing me earlier. I ducked in here to escape them. It'd be nice to get back to work without being jostled.'

'No problem,' he said. 'I'm heading that way anyway.'

Leandro walked beside Miranda on the way back to the gallery. He was always struck by how tiny she was. Built like a ballerina with fine limbs and an elfin face, with big tawny-brown eyes and auburn hair, yet her skin was without a single freckle—it was as white and pure as Devon cream. She had an ethereal beauty about her. She reminded him of a fairy-tale character—an innocent waif lost in the middle of a crazy out-of-control world.

Seeing her hiding in that café had tripped a switch inside his head. It was like he'd had a brain snap. He hadn't thought it through but it seemed…*right* some-how. She needed a bolthole and he needed someone to help him sort out the mess his father had left behind. Maybe it would've been better to commission some-one local. Maybe he could have sold the lot without proper valuation. Hell, he didn't really know why he had asked her, except he knew she was having a tough time of it with her father's love-child scandal still doing the rounds.

That and the fact he couldn't bear the thought of being in that villa on his own with only the ghosts of the past to haunt him. He hadn't been back since the day he'd left when he was eight years old.

It wasn't like him to act so impulsively but seeing Miranda hiding behind that pot plant had made him re-alise how stressed she was about her father's latest pec-cadillo. He had heard from her brothers the press had camped outside her flat for the last month. She hadn't been able to take a step without a camera or a micro-phone being shoved in her face. Being the daughter of famous celebrities came with a heavy price tag. Or, at least, it did for her.

Leandro had always felt a little sorry for Miranda. She was constantly compared to her flamboyant and glamorous mother and found lacking. Now she was being compared to her half-sister. Kat Winwood *was* stunning. No two ways about that. Kat was the bill-board-beautiful type. Kat would stop traffic. Air traf-fic. Miranda's beauty was quiet, the sort of beauty that grew on you. And she was shy in an endearingly old-fashioned way. He didn't know too many women who blushed as easily as her. She never flirted. And she never dated. Not since she had lost her first and only boyfriend to leukaemia when she was sixteen. Leandro couldn't help admiring her loyalty, even if he privately thought she was throwing her life away.

But who was he to judge?

He hadn't got any plans for happy-ever-after either.

Miranda was the best person to advise him on his father's collection. Of course she was. She was reliable and sensible. She was competent and efficient and she had an excellent eye. She had helped her brother Julius buy some great pieces at various auctions. She could spot a fraud at twenty paces. It would only take a week or two to sort out the collection and he would be doing her a favour in the process.

But there was one thing she didn't know about him.

He hadn't even told Julius or Jake about Rosie.

It was why he had gone to his father's funeral alone. Going back to Nice had been like ripping open a wound.

There'd been numerous times when he could have mentioned it. He could have told his two closest friends the tragic secret he carried like a shackle around his heart. But instead he had let everyone think he was an only child. Every time he thought of his baby sister his chest would seize. The thought of her little chubby face with its dimpled, sunny smile would bring his guilt crashing down on him like a guillotine.

For all these years he had said nothing. To anyone. He had left that part of his life—his former life, his childhood—back in France. His life was divided into two sections: France and England. Before and After. Sometimes that 'before' life felt like a bad dream—a horrible, blood-chilling nightmare. But then he would wake up and realise with a sickening twist of his gut that it was true. Inescapably, heartbreakingly true. It didn't matter where he lived. How far he travelled. How hard he worked to block the memories. The guilt came with him. It sat on his shoulder during the day. It poked him awake at night. It drove vicious needles through his skull until he was blind with pain.

Speaking about his family was torture for him. Pure, unadulterated torture. He hated even thinking about it. He didn't have a family.

His family had been blown apart twenty-seven years ago and *he* had been the one to do it.

CHAPTER TWO

'YOU'RE GOING TO FRANCE?' Jasmine Connelly said, eyes wide with sparkling intrigue. 'With Leandro Allegretti?'

Miranda had dropped into Jasmine's bridal boutique in Mayfair for a quick catch-up before she flew out the following day. Jaz was sewing Swarovski crystals onto a gorgeous wedding dress, the sort of dress for every girl who dreamed of being a princess. Miranda had pictured a dress just like it back in the day when her life had been going according to plan. Now every time she saw a wedding dress she felt sad.

'Not going *with* him as such,' she said, absently fingering the fabric of the wedding gown on the mannequin. 'I'm meeting him over there to help him sort out his father's art collection.'

'When do you go?'

'Tomorrow… For a couple of weeks.'

'Should be interesting,' Jaz said with a smile in her voice.

Miranda looked at her with a frown. 'Why do you say that?'

Jaz gave her a worldly look. 'Come, now. Don't you ever notice the way he looks at you?'

Miranda felt something unhitch in her chest. 'He never looks at me. He barely even says a word to me. This is the first time we've exchanged more than a couple of sentences.'

'Clues, my dear Watson,' Jaz said with a cheeky smile. 'I've seen the way he looks at you when he thinks no one's watching. I reckon if it weren't for his relationship with your family he would act on it. You'd better pack some decent underwear just in case he changes his mind.'

Miranda pointedly ignored her friend's teasing comment as she trailed her hand through the voluminous veil hanging beside the dress. 'Do you know much about his private life?'

Jaz stopped sewing to look at her with twinkling grey-blue eyes. 'So you are interested. Yay! I thought the day would never come.'

Miranda frowned. 'I know what you're thinking but you couldn't be more wrong. I'm not the least bit interested in him or anyone. I just wondered if he had a current girlfriend, that's all.'

'Not that I've heard of, but you know how close he keeps his cards,' Jaz said. 'He could have a string of women on the go. He is, after all, one of Jake's mates.'

Every time Jaz said Jake's name her mouth got a snarly, contemptuous look. The enmity between them was ongoing. It had started when Jaz was sixteen at one of Miranda's parents' legendary New Year's Eve parties. Jaz refused to be drawn on what had actually happened in Jake's bedroom that night. Jake too kept tight-lipped. But it was common knowledge he despised Jaz and made every effort to avoid her if he could.

Miranda glanced at the glittering diamond on her friend's ring finger. It was Jaz's third engagement and, while Miranda didn't exactly dislike Jaz's latest fiancé, Myles, she didn't think he was 'The One' for her. Not that she could ever say that to Jaz. Jaz didn't take too kindly to being told what she didn't want to hear. Miranda had had the same misgivings over Fiancés One and Two. She just had to hope and trust her headstrong and stubborn friend would realise how she was short-changing herself before the wedding actually took place.

Jaz stood back and cast a critical eye over her handiwork. 'What do you think?'

'It's beautiful,' Miranda said with a sigh.

'Yeah, well, I'm going cross-eyed with all these crystals,' Jaz said. 'I've got to get it done so I can start on Holly's. She's awfully nice, isn't she?'

'Gorgeous,' Miranda said. 'It's amazing, seeing Julius so happy. To tell you the truth, I wasn't sure he was ever going to fall in love. They're total opposites and yet they're so perfect for each other.'

Jaz looked at her with her head on one side, that teasing glint back in her gaze. 'Is that a note of wistfulness I can hear?'

Miranda rearranged her features. 'I'd better get going.' She grabbed her tote bag, slung it over her shoulder and leaned in to kiss Jaz on the cheek. 'See you when I get back.'

* * *

When Miranda landed in Nice she saw Leandro waiting for her in the terminal. He was dressed more casually this time but if anything it made him look even more heart-stoppingly attractive. The dark blue denim jeans clung to his leanly muscled legs. The rolled back sleeves of his light blue shirt highlighted his deep tan and emphasised the masculinity of the dark hair liberally sprinkled over his strong forearms. He was cleanly shaven but she could see where he had nicked himself on the left side of his jaw. For some reason, it humanised him. He was always so well put together, so in control. Was being back in his childhood home unsettling for him? Upsetting? What emotions were going on behind the dark screen of his eyes?

As he caught her eye a flutter of awareness rippled deep and low in her belly. Would he kiss her in greeting? She couldn't remember him ever touching her. Not even by accident. Even when he'd walked her back to the gallery last week he had kept his distance. There had been no shoulder brushing. Not that she even reached his shoulders. She was five-foot-five to his six-foot-three.

Miranda smiled shyly as he came towards her. 'Hi.'

'Hello.' Was it her imagination or was his voice deeper and huskier than normal? The sound of it moved over her skin as if he had reached out and stroked her. But he kept a polite distance, although she couldn't help noticing his gaze slipped to her mouth for the briefest moment. 'How was your flight?' he said.

'Lovely,' she said. 'But you didn't have to put me in first class. I was happy to fly coach.'

He took her carry-on bag from her, somehow without touching her fingers as he did so. 'I didn't want anyone bothering you,' he said. 'There's nothing worse than being a captive audience to someone's life story.'

Miranda gave a light laugh. 'True.'

She followed him out to the car park where he opened the door of the hire car for her. She couldn't fault his manners, but then, he had always been a gentleman. She had never known him to be anything but polite and considerate. She wondered if this was difficult for him, coming back to France to his early childhood home. What memories did it stir for him? Did it make him wish he had been closer to his father? Did it stir up regrets that now it was too late?

She glanced at him as they left the car park and joined the traffic on the Promenade des Anglais that followed the brilliant blue of the coastline of the Mediterranean Sea. He was frowning as usual; even his hands on the steering wheel were clenched. She could see the tanned flesh straining over his knuckles. The line of his jaw was grim. Everything about him was tense, wound up like a spring. It looked like he was in physical pain.

'Are you okay?' she asked.

He looked at her briefly, moving his lips in a grimace-like smile that didn't reveal his teeth. 'I'm fine.'

Miranda didn't buy it for a second. 'Have you got one of your headaches?' She had seen him once at Ravensdene when he had come down with a migraine.

He was always so strong and fit that to see him rendered helpless with such pain and sickness had been an awful shock. The doctor had had to be called to give him a strong painkiller injection. Jake had driven him back to London the next day, as he had still been too ill to drive himself.

'Just a tension headache,' he said. 'Nothing I can't handle.'

'When did you arrive?'

'Yesterday,' he said. 'I had a job to finish in Stockholm.'

'I expect it must be difficult coming back,' Miranda said, still watching him. 'Emotional for you, I mean. Did you ever come back after your parents divorced?'

'No.'

She frowned. 'Not even to visit your father?'

His hands tightened another notch on the steering wheel. 'We didn't have that sort of relationship.'

Miranda wondered how his father could have been so cold and distant. How could a man turn his back on his son—his only child—just because his marriage had broken up? Surely the bond of parenthood was much stronger than that? Her parents had gone through a bitter divorce before she'd been born and, while they hadn't been around much due to their theatre commitments, as far as she could tell Julius and Jake had never doubted they were loved.

'Your father doesn't sound like a very nice person,' she said. 'Was he always a drinker? I'm sorry. Maybe you don't want to talk about it. It's just, Julius told me you didn't like it when your father came to London to see you. He said your dad embarrassed you by getting horribly drunk.'

Leandro's gaze was focussed on the clogging traffic ahead but she could see the way his jaw was locked down, as if tightened by a clamp. 'He didn't always drink that heavily.'

'What made him start? The divorce?'

He didn't answer for a moment. 'It certainly didn't help.'

Miranda wondered about the dynamics of his parents' relationship and how each of them had handled the breakdown of their marriage. Some men found the loss of a relationship far more devastating than others. Some sank into depression, others quickly re-partnered to avoid being alone. The news was regularly full of horrid stories of men getting back at their ex-wives after a broken relationship—cruel and vindictive attempts to get revenge, sometimes involving the children, with tragic results. 'Did he ever remarry?' she asked.

'No.'

'Did he have other partners?'

'Occasionally, but not for long,' Leandro said. 'He was difficult to live with. There were few women who would put up with him.'

'So it was his fault your mother left him?' Miranda asked. 'Because he was so difficult to live with?'

He didn't answer for so long she thought he hadn't heard her over the noise of the traffic outside. 'No,' he said heavily. 'That was my fault.'

Miranda looked at him in shock. '*You?* Why would

you think that? That's ridiculous. You were only eight years old. Why on earth would you blame yourself?'

He gave her an unreadable glance before he took a left turn. 'My father's place is a few blocks up here. Have you ever been to Nice before?'

'A couple of years ago—but don't try and change the subject,' she said. 'Why do you blame yourself for your parents' divorce?'

'Don't all kids blame themselves?'

Miranda thought about it for a moment. Her mother had said a number of times how having twins had put pressure on her relationship with her father. But then, Elisabetta wasn't a naturally maternal type. She was happiest when the attention was on her, not on her children. Miranda had felt that keenly as she'd been growing up. All of her friends—apart from Jaz—were envious of her having a glamorous showbiz mother. And Elisabetta could *act* like a wonderful mother when it suited her.

It was the times when she didn't that hurt Miranda the most.

But why did Leandro think *he* was responsible for his parents' break-up? Had *they* told him that? Had they made him feel guilty? What sort of parents had they been to do something so reprehensible? How could they make a young child feel responsible for the breakdown of a marriage? That was the adults' responsibility, not a child's, and certainly not a young child's.

But she didn't pursue the conversation for at that point Leandro pulled into the driveway of a rundown-looking villa in the Belle Epoqué style. At first she thought he must have made a mistake, pulled into the wrong driveway or something. The place was like something out of a gothic noir film. The outside of the three-storey-high building was charcoal-grey with the stain of years of carbon monoxide pollution. The windows with the ragged curtains drawn were like closed eyes.

The villa was like a faded Hollywood star. Miranda could see the golden era of glamour in its lead-roofed cupolas on the corners and the ornamental ironwork and flamboyance of the stucco decorations that resembled a wedding cake.

But it had been sadly neglected. She knew many of the grand villas of the Belle Époque era along the Promenade des Anglais had not survived urban redevelopment. But the extravagance of the period was still apparent in this old beauty.

It made Miranda's blood tick in her veins. What a gorgeous old place for Leandro to inherit. It was a piece of history. A relic from an enchanted time when the aristocracy had flaunted their wealth by hiring architects to design opulent villas with every imaginable embellishment: faux stonework, figureheads, frescos, friezes, decorative ironwork, ornamental stucco work, cupolas, painted effects, garlands and grotesques. The aristocracy had indulged their taste for the exotic, with Italian and Classic influences as well as Gothic, Eastern and Moorish.

And he was packing it up and *selling* it?

Miranda looked up at him as he opened her car door for her. 'Leandro, it's amazing! What a glorious building. It's like a time capsule from the Art Nouveau period. This was your childhood home? *Really?*'

He clearly didn't share her excitement for the building. His expression had that closed-off look about it, as shuttered as the windows of the villa they were about to enter. 'It's very run-down,' he said.

'Yes, but it can be brought back to life.' Miranda beamed at him, clasping her hands in excitement. 'I'm so glad you asked me to come. I can't wait to see what's inside.'

He stepped forward to unlock the door with the set of keys he was holding in his hand. 'Dust and cobwebs mostly.'

Miranda's gaze went to his tanned hand, that funny fluttery feeling passing over the floor of her belly as she watched the way his long, strong fingers turned the key in the lock. Who was the last woman he'd touched with those arrantly masculine but beautiful hands? Were his hands smooth or rough or something deliciously in between? She couldn't stop herself from imagining those strong, capable hands exploring female flesh. Caressing a breast. Gliding down a smooth thigh. Touching the silken skin between her legs.

Her legs?

Miranda jerked back from her wayward thoughts as if a hand had grabbed and pulled on the back of her clothing. What was she doing thinking of him that way? She didn't think of *any* man that way.

That way was over for her.

It had died with Mark. She owed it to his memory, to all he had meant to her and she to him.

Miranda could not allow herself to think of moving on with her life. Of having a life. A normal life. Her dreams of normal were gone.

Dead and buried.

Leandro glanced at her. 'What's wrong?'

Miranda felt her face flame. Why did she always act like a flustered schoolgirl when she was around him? She was an adult, for God's sake. She had to act mature and sensible. Cool and in charge of her emotions and her traitorous needs. She could do that. *Of course she could.* 'Erm…nothing.'

His frown created a deep crevasse between his brows. 'Would you rather go to a hotel? There's one a couple of blocks down. I could—'

'No, of course not.' She painted on a bright smile. 'Don't spoil it for me by insisting I stay at some plush hotel. This is right up my alley. I want to be in amongst the dust and cobwebs. Who knows what priceless treasures are hidden inside?'

Something moved at the back of his gaze, as quick as the twitch of a curtain. But then his expression went back to its default position. 'Come this way,' he said.

Miranda followed him into the villa, her heels echoing on the marbled floor of the grand foyer. It made her feel she was stepping into a vacuum, moving back in time. Thousands of dust motes rose in the air, the sunlight catching them where it was slanting in from the windows either side of the opulently carved and sweeping staircase.

As Leandro closed the door, the central chandelier

tinkled above them as the draught of the outside air breathed against its glittering crystals.

Miranda felt a rush of goose bumps scamper over every inch of her flesh. She turned a full circle, taking in the bronze, marble and onyx statues positioned about the foyer. There were paintings on every wall, portraits and landscapes from the seventeenth and eighteenth centuries; some looked even older. It was like stepping into a neglected museum. A thick layer of dust was over everything like a ghostly shroud.

'Wow...' she breathed in wonder.

Leandro merely looked bored. 'I'll show you to your room first. Then I'll give you the guided tour.'

Miranda followed him upstairs, having to restrain herself from stopping in front of every painting or *objet d'art* on the way past. She caught tantalising glimpses of the second floor rooms through the open doors; most of the furniture was draped with dust sheets but even so she could see in times gone past the villa had been a showcase for grandeur and wealth. There were a couple of rooms with the doors closed. One she assumed was Leandro's bedroom but she knew it wasn't the master suite as they had passed it three doors back. Did he not want to occupy the room his father had slept in all those years?

Miranda felt another prickle of goose bumps.

Had his father perhaps *died* in there?

Thankfully the room Leandro had assigned her had been aired. The faded formal curtains had been pulled back and secured by the brass fittings and the window opened so fresh air could circulate. The breeze was playing with the gossamer-sheer fabric of the curtain in little billowy puffs and sighs.

'I hope the bed's comfortable,' Leandro said as he placed her bag on a velvet-topped chest at the foot of the bed. 'The linen is fresh. I bought some new stuff when I got here yesterday.'

Miranda glanced at him. 'Did your father die at home?'

His brows came together. 'Why do you ask?'

She gave a little shrug, absently rubbing her upper arms with her crossed-over hands. 'Just wondering.'

He held her look for a beat before turning away, one of his hands scoring a pathway through the thickness of his hair. 'He was found unconscious by a neighbour and died a few hours later in hospital.'

'So you didn't get to say goodbye to him?'

He made a sound of derision. 'We said our good-byes a long time ago.'

Miranda looked at the landscape of his face—the strong jaw, the tight mouth with its lines of tension running down each side and the shadowed eyes. 'What happened between the two of you?' she said.

His eyes moved away from hers. 'I'll leave you to unpack. The bathroom is through there. I'll be down-stairs in the study.'

'Leandro?'

He stopped at the door and she heard him release a 'what now?' breath before he turned to look at her with dark eyes that flashed with unmistakable irritation. 'You're not here to give me grief counselling, okay?'

Miranda opened her eyes a little wider at his acerbic tone. She had never seen him even mildly angry before. He was always so emotionless, so neutral and blank…apart from that frown, of course. 'I'm sorry. I didn't mean to upset you.'

He scrubbed his hand over his face as he let out another whoosh of air. 'I'm sorry,' he said in a weighted tone. 'That was uncalled for.'

'It's fine,' she said. 'I realise this is a difficult time for you.'

His mouth twisted but it was nowhere near a smile, not even a quarter of one. 'Let me know if you need anything. I'm not used to catering for guests. I might've overlooked something.'

'Don't you have visitors come and stay with you at your place in London?' Miranda said.

His eyes were as unfathomable as ever as they held hers. 'Women, you mean?'

Miranda felt another blush storm into her cheeks. Why on earth was she was discussing his sex life with him? It was crossing a boundary she had never crossed before. She'd thought about him with other women. Many times. How could she not? She'd seen the way other women looked at him. The way their eyes flared in interest. The way they licked their lips and fluttered their eyelashes, or moved or preened their bodies so he would take notice. She had been witnessing his effect on women for as long as she could remember. He wasn't just eye candy. He was an eye banquet. He was intelligent, sophisticated, cultured and wealthy to boot. Alpha, but without the arrogance. He was everything a woman would want in a sexual partner. He was the stuff of fantasies. Hot, erotic fantasies she never allowed herself to have. What did it matter to her what he did or who he did it with?

She didn't want to know.

Well, maybe just a little.

'You do have them occasionally, don't you?' Miranda said.

One of his dark brows rose in a quizzical arc. '*Have* them?'

She held his look but it took an enormous effort. Her cheeks were on fire. Hot enough to sear a steak. He was teasing her. She could see a tiny glint in the dark chocolate of his eyes. Even one corner of his mouth had lifted a fraction. He was making her out to be a prude who couldn't talk about sex openly. Why did everyone automatically assume because she was celibate she was uptight about all things sexual? That she was some old-world throwback who couldn't handle modernity? 'You know exactly what I'm talking about so stop trying to embarrass me.'

His eyes didn't waver from hers. 'I'm not a monk.'

Miranda couldn't stop her mind running off with *that* information. Picturing him with women. Being very un-monk-like with them. Touching them, kissing them, making love to them. She imagined his body naked—the toned, tanned and taut perfection of him in the throes of animal passion.

She could feel her own body stirring in excitement, her pulse kicking up its pace, her blood pulsing with the primitive drumbeat of lust, her inner core contracting with a delicious clench of desire. She quickly moistened her lips with the point of her tongue, an electric jolt of awareness zapping her as she saw his dark-as-night gaze follow every micro-millimetre of its pathway across her mouth.

The subtle change in atmosphere made the air suddenly super-charged. She could feel the voltage crackling in the silence like a singing wire.

He was standing at least two metres away and yet she felt as if he had touched her. Her lips buzzed and fizzed. Throbbed. *Ached.* Would he kiss soft and slow or hard and fast? Would his stubble scrape or graze her? What would he taste of? Salty or sweet? Good quality coffee or top-shelf wine? Testosterone-rich man in his prime?

Miranda became aware of her body shifting. Stirring. Sensing. It felt like every cell was unfurling from a tightly wound ball. Her body stretched its cramped limbs like a long-confined creature. Her frozen blood thawed, warmed, heated. Sizzled.

Needs she had long ignored pulsed. Each little ripple of want in her inner core reminded her: she was a woman. He was a man. They were alone in a big, run-down old house with no one as buffer. No older brothers. No servants. No distractions.

No chaperone.

'I hope it won't cramp your style, having me here,' Miranda said with what she hoped was suitably cool poise.

There was little to read on Leandro's face except for the kindling heat in his gaze as it continued to

hold hers. 'So you wouldn't mind if I brought someone home with me?'

Oh, dear God, *would* he? Would he bring someone
back here? Would she have to watch some gorgeous
woman drape herself all over him? Would she have to
watch as they simpered up at him? Flirted and fussed
over him? Would she have to go to bed knowing that,
only a few thin walls and doors away, he was doing all
sorts of wickedly sensual, un-monk-like things with
someone else?

Miranda lifted her chin. 'Just because I've sworn
a vow of celibacy doesn't mean I expect those around
me to follow my example.'

He studied her for an infinitesimal moment, his eyes
going back and forth between each of hers in an assessing manner that was distinctly unnerving. Why
was he looking at her like that? What was he seeing?
Did he sense her body's reaction to his? She was doing
her level best to conceal the effect he had on her but
she knew most body language was unconscious. She
had already licked her lips three times. *Three times!*

'Do you think Mark would've sacrificed his life like
you're doing if the tables were turned?' he said at last.

Miranda pursed her lips. *At least it would stop her
licking them*, she thought. She knew exactly where
this was going. Her brothers were always banging on
about it. Jaz, too, would offer her opinion on how she
was missing out on the best years of her life, yadda-
yadda-yadda.

'I'll make a deal with you, Leandro,' she said, eye-

MELANIE MILBURNE 39

balling him. 'I won't tell you how to live your life if you don't tell me how to live mine.'

His mouth took on a rueful slant. 'Put those kitten claws away, *cara*,' he said. 'I don't need any more enemies.'

He had never used a term of endearment when addressing her before. The way he said it, with that hint of an Italian accent all those years living in England hadn't quite removed, made her spine tingle. But why was he addressing her like that other than to tease her? To mock her?

Miranda threw him a reproachful look. 'Don't patronise me. I'm an adult. I know my own mind.'

'But you were just a kid back then,' he said. 'If he'd lived you would've broken up within a couple of months, if not weeks. It's what teenagers do.'

'That's not true,' Miranda said. 'We'd been friends since we were little kids. We were in love. We were soul mates. We planned to spend the rest of our lives together.'

He shook his head at her as if she was talking utter nonsense. 'Do you really believe that? Come on. *Really?*'

Miranda aligned her spine. Straightened her shoulders. Steeled her resolve to deflect any criticism of her decision to remain committed to the promises she had made to Mark. She and Mark had become close friends during early childhood when they had gone to the same small village school before she'd been sent to boarding school with Jaz. They'd officially started dating at fourteen. Her friendship with Mark had been longer than that with Jaz who had come to Ravensdene when she was eight.

Along with Mark's steady friendship, his stable home life had been a huge draw and comfort for Miranda. His parents were so normal compared to hers. There'd been no high-flying parties with Hollywood superstars and theatre royalty coming and going all hours of the day and night. In the Redbank household there'd been no tempestuous outbursts with door-slamming and insults hurled, and no passionate making up that would only last a week or two before the cycle would begin again.

Mark's parents, James and Susanne, were supportive and nurturing of each other and Mark and had always made Miranda feel like a part of the family. They actually took the time to listen to any problems she had. They were never too busy. They didn't judge or dismiss her or even tell her what to do. They listened.

Leandro had no right to doubt her convictions. No right to criticise her choices. She had made up her mind and nothing he or anyone could say or do would make her veer from the course her conscience had taken. 'Of course I do,' she said. 'I believe it with all my heart.'

The humming silence tiptoed from each corner of the room.

Leandro kept looking at her in that measuring way. Unsettling her. Making her think of things she had no right to be thinking. Erotic things. Forbidden things. Like how his mouth would feel against hers. How his hands would feel against her flesh. How their bodies would fit together—her slight curves against his toned male hardness. How it would feel to glide her mouth along his stubbly jaw, to press her lips to his and open her mouth to the searching thrust of his tongue.

She had never had such a rush of wicked thoughts before. They were running amok, making a mockery of her convictions. Making her aware of the needs she had for so long pretended weren't there. Needs that were moving within that dark, secret place in her body. The way he was looking at her made her ache with unspent passion. She tried to control every micro-expression on her face. Stood as still as one of his father's cold, lifeless statues downstairs.

But, as if he had seen enough to satisfy him, he finally broke the silence. 'I'll be in the study downstairs. We'll eat out once you've unpacked. Give me a shout once you're done.'

Miranda blinked. Dining out? With him? In public? People would assume they were dating. What if someone took a photo and it got back to Mark's parents? Even though they had said—along with everyone else—she should get on with her life, she knew they would find it heartbreakingly difficult to watch her do so. How could they not? Everything she did with someone else would make their loss all the more painful. Mark had been their only son. Their only child. The dreams and hopes they'd had for him had died with him. The milestones of life: dating, engagement, marriage and children would be salt ground into an open wound.

She couldn't do it to them.

'You don't want me to fix something for us here?' Miranda said.

Leandro gave a soft sound that could have been his version of a laugh. 'You're getting your fairy tales mixed up,' he said. 'You're Sleeping Beauty, not Cinderella.'

Miranda felt a wick of anger light up inside her. What right did he have to mock her choice to remain loyal to Mark's memory? 'Is this why you've asked me here? So you can make fun of me?'

'I'm not making fun of you.'

'Then what *are* you doing?'

His gaze dipped to her mouth for a nanosecond before meshing with hers once more. 'I have absolutely no idea.'

Miranda frowned. 'What do you mean?'

He came over to where she was standing. He stopped within a foot of her but even so she could feel the magnetic pull of his body as she lifted her gaze to his. She had never been this close to him. Not front to front. Almost toe to toe.

Her breathing halted as he placed a gentle but firm fingertip to the underside of her chin, lifting her face so her eyes had no possible way of escaping the mesmerising power of his. She could feel the slow burn of his touch, each individual whorl of his blunt fingertip like an electrode against her skin. She could smell the woodsy and citrus fragrance of his aftershave—not heady or overpowering, but subtle, with tantalising grace notes of lemon and lime.

She could see the dark pinpricks of his regrowth

along his jaw, a heady reminder of the potency of his male hormones charging through his body. She could feel her own hormones doing cartwheels.

Her tongue sneaked out before she could stop it, leaving a layer of much-needed moisture over her lips. His gaze honed in on her mouth, his eyelashes at half-mast over his dark-as-pitch eyes.

Something fell off a high shelf in her stomach as his thumb brushed over her lower lip. The grazing movement of his thumb against the sensitive skin of her mouth made every nerve sit up and take notice. She could feel them twirling, pirouetting, in a frenzy of traitorous excitement.

His large, warm hand gently slid along the curve of her cheek, cupping one side of her face, some of her hair falling against the back of his hand like a silk curtain.

Had *anyone* ever held her like this? Tenderly cradled her face as if it were something delicate and priceless? The warmth of his palm seared her flesh, making her ache for him to cup not just her face but her breasts, to feel his firm male skin against her softer one.

'I shouldn't have brought you here,' he said in a deep, gravelly tone that sent another shockwave across the base of her belly.

A hummingbird was trapped inside the cavity of Miranda's chest, fluttering frantically inside each of the four chambers of her heart. 'Why?' Her voice was barely much more than a squeak.

He moved his thumb in a back-and-forth motion

over her cheek, his inscrutable eyes holding her prisoner. 'There are things you don't know about me.'

Miranda swallowed. What didn't she know? Did he have bodies buried in the cellar? Leather whips and chains and handcuffs? A red room? 'Wh-what things?'

'Not the things you're thinking.'

'I'm not thinking those things.'

He smiled a crooked half-smile that had mockery at its core. 'Sweet, innocent, Miranda,' he said. 'The little girl in a woman's body who refuses to grow up.'

Miranda stepped out of his hold, rubbing at her cheek in a pointed manner. 'I thought I was here to look at your father's art collection. I'm sorry if that seems terribly naïve of me but I've never had any reason not to trust you before now.'

'You can trust me.'

She chanced a look at him again. His expression had lost its mocking edge. If anything he looked…sad. She could see the pained lines across his forehead, the shadows in his eyes, the grim set to his mouth. 'Why am I here, Leandro?' Somehow her voice had come out whispery instead of strident and firm.

He let out a long breath. 'Because when I saw you in London I… I don't know what I thought. I saw you cowering behind that pot plant and—'

'I wasn't cowering,' Miranda put in indignantly. 'I was hiding.'

'I felt sorry for you.'

The silence echoed for a moment with his bald statement.

Miranda drew in a tight breath. 'So you rescued me

by pretending to need me to sort out your father's collection. Is there even a collection?'

'Yes.'

'Then maybe you'd better show it to me.'

'Come this way.'

Miranda followed him out of the suite and back downstairs to a room next door to the larger of the two sitting rooms. Leandro opened the door and gestured for her to go in. She stepped past him in the doorway, acutely conscious of the way his shirt sleeve brushed against her arm. Every nerve stood up and took notice. Every fine hair tingled at the roots. It was like his body was emitting waves of electricity and she had only to step over an invisible boundary to feel the full force of it.

The atmosphere inside the room was airless and musty, as if it had been closed up a long time. It was packed with canvasses, on the walls, and others wrapped and stacked in leaning piles against the shrouded furniture.

Miranda sent her gaze over the paintings on the walls, examining each one with her trained apprentice's eye. Even without her qualifications and experience she'd have been able to see this was a collection of enormous value. One of the landscapes was certainly a Gainsborough, or if not a very credible imitation. What other treasures were hidden underneath those wrapped canvasses?

Miranda turned to look at Leandro. 'This is amazing. But I'm not sure I'm experienced enough to handle such a large collection. We'd need to ship the pieces back to London for proper valuation. It's too much for one person to deal with. Some of these pieces could be worth hundreds of thousands of pounds, maybe even millions. You might want to keep some as an investment. Sell them in a few years so you can—'

'I don't want them.'

She frowned at his implacable tone. 'But that's crazy, Leandro. You could have your own collection. You could have it on show at a private museum. It would be—'

'I have no interest in making money out of my father's collection,' he said. 'Just do what you have to do. I'll pay for any shipment costs but that's as far as I'm prepared to go.'

Miranda watched open-mouthed as he strode out of the room, the dust motes he'd disturbed hovering in the ringing silence.

CHAPTER THREE

LEANDRO WORKED THE floor of his father's study like a lion trapped in a cat carrier. It had been a mistake to bring Miranda here. Here to the epicentre of his pain and anguish. He should have sold the collection without consulting anyone. What did it matter if those wretched paintings were valuable? They weren't valuable to him. Making money out of his father's legacy seemed immoral somehow to him. He didn't understand why his father had left everything to him.

Over the last few years their relationship had deteriorated to perfunctory calls at Christmas or birthdays. Most of the time his father would be heavily inebriated, his words slurred, his memory skewed. It had been all Leandro could do to listen to his father's drunken ramblings knowing *he* had been the one to cause the destruction of his father's life. Surely his father had known how difficult this trip back here would be? Had he done it to twist the knife? To force him to face what he had spent the last two decades avoiding? Everything in this run-down villa represented the misery of his father's life—a life spent drinking himself to oblivion so he could forget the tragedy of the past.

The tragedy Leandro had caused.

He looked out of the window that overlooked the garden at the back of the villa. He hadn't been able to bring himself to go out there yet. It had once been a spectacular affair with neatly trimmed hedges, flowering shrubs and borders filled with old-world roses whose heady scent would fill the air. It had been a magical place for he and his sister to scamper about and play hide and seek in amongst the cool, green shaded laneways of the hedges.

But now it was an overgrown mess of weeds, misshapen hedges and skeletal rose bushes with one or two half-hearted blooms. Parts of the garden were so overrun they couldn't be seen properly from the house.

It reminded Leandro of his father's life—sad, neglected, abused and abandoned. Wasted.

How could he have thought to bring Miranda here? How long before she discovered Rosie's room? He couldn't keep it locked up for ever. Stepping in there was like stepping back in time. It was painfully surreal. Everything was exactly the same as the day Rosie had disappeared from the beach. Every toy. Every doll. Every childish scribble she had ever done. Every messy and colourful finger-painting. Every article of clothing left in the wardrobe as if she were going to come back and use it. Even her hairbrush was on the dressing table with some of her silky dark-brown hairs still trapped in the bristles—a haunting reminder of the last time it had been used.

Even the striped towel they had been sitting on at the beach was there on the foot of the child-sized princess bed. The bed Rosie had been so proud of after moving out of her cot. Her 'big-girl bed', she'd called it. He still remembered her excited little face as she'd told him how she had chosen it with their mother while he'd been at school.

It was a lifetime ago.

Why had his father left the room intact for so long? Had he wanted Leandro to see it? Was that why he'd left him the villa and its contents? Knowing Leandro would have to come in and pack up every single item of Rosie's? Why hadn't his father seen to it himself or got someone impartial to do it? It had been twenty-seven years, for pity's sake. There was no possibility of Rosie ever coming home. The police had been blunt with his parents once the first few months had passed with no leads, no evidence, no clues and no tip-offs.

Leandro had seen the statistics. Rosie had joined the thousands of people who went missing without trace. Every single day families across the globe were shattered by the disappearance of a loved one. They were left with the stomach-churning dread of wondering what had happened to their beloved family member. Praying they were still alive but deep down knowing such miracles were rare. Wondering if they had suffered or were still suffering. It was cruel torture not to know and yet just as bad speculating.

Leandro had spent every year of his life since wondering. Praying. Begging. Pleading with a God he no longer believed in—if he ever had. Rosie wasn't coming back. She was gone and he was responsible.

The guilt he felt over Rosie's disappearance was a band around his chest that would tighten every time he saw a toddler. Rosie had been with him on the pebbly beach when he was six and she was three. He could recall her cute little chubby-cheeked face and starfish dimpled hands with such clarity he felt like it was yesterday. For years he'd kept thinking the life he was living since was just a bad dream. That he would wake up and there would be Rosie with her sunny smile sitting on the striped towel next to him. But every time he would wake and he would feel that crushing hammer blow of guilt.

His mother had stepped a few feet away to an ice-cream vendor, leaving Leandro in charge. When she'd come back, Rosie had gone. Vanished. Snatched from where she had been sitting. The beach had been scoured. The water searched. The police had interviewed hundreds of beach-goers but there was no sign of Rosie. No one had seen anything suspicious. Leandro had only turned his back for a moment or two to look at a speedboat that was going past. When he'd turned around he'd seen his mother coming towards him with two ice-cream cones; her face had contorted in horror when she'd seen the empty space on the towel beside him.

He had never forgotten that look on his mother's face. Every time he saw his mother he remembered it. It haunted him. Tortured him.

His parents' marriage hadn't been strong in the first

place. Losing Rosie had gouged open cracks that were already there. The divorce had been bitter and painful two years after Rosie's disappearance. His father hadn't wanted custody of Leandro. He hadn't even asked for visitation rights. His mother hadn't wanted him either. But she must have known people would judge her harshly if she didn't take him with her when she went back to her homeland, England. Mothers were meant to love their children.

But how could his mother love him when he was responsible for the loss of her adored baby girl?

Not that his mother ever blamed him. Not openly. Not in words. It was the looks that told him what she thought. His father's too. Those looks said, *why weren't you watching her?* As the years went on his father had begun to verbalise it. The blame would come pouring out after he'd been on one of his binges. But it was nothing Leandro hadn't already heard echoing in his head. Day after day, week after week…for years now the same accusing voice would keep him awake at night. It would give him nightmares. He would wake with a jolt and remember the awful truth.

There wasn't a day that went past that he didn't think of his sister. Ever since that gut-wrenching day he would look for her in the crowd, hoping to catch a glimpse of her. Hoping that whoever had taken her had not done so for nefarious reasons, but had taken her to fulfil a wish to have a child and had loved and cared for her since. He couldn't bear to think of her coming to harm. He couldn't bear to think of her lying cold in some grisly shallow grave, her little body bruised and broken. As the years had gone on he imagined her growing up. He looked for an older version of her. She would be thirty now.

In his good dreams she would be married with children of her own by now.

In his nightmares…

He closed the door on his torturous imaginings. For twenty-seven years he had lived with this incessant agony. The agony of not knowing. The agony of being responsible for losing her. The agony of knowing he had ruined his parents' lives.

He could never forgive himself.

He didn't even bother trying.

Miranda spent an hour looking over the collection, carefully uncovering the canvasses to get an idea of what she was dealing with. Apart from some of the obvious fakes, most of the collection would have to be shipped back to England for proper evaluation. The paintings needed to be x-rayed in order to establish how they were composed. Infrared imaging would then be used to see the original drawings and painting losses, and Raman spectroscopy would determine the identity of the varnish. It would take a team of experts far more qualified and experienced than her to bring all of these works to their former glory. But she couldn't help feeling touched Leandro had asked her to be the first to run her eyes over the collection.

Why *had* he done that?

Had it simply been an impulsive thing, as he had intimated, or had he truly thought she was the best one to do it? Whatever his reasons, it was like being let in on a secret. He had opened a part of his life that no one else had had access to before.

It was sad to think of Leandro's father living here on his own for years. It looked like no maintenance had been done for a decade, if not longer. Cobwebs hung from every corner. The dust was so thick she could feel it irritating her nostrils. Every time she moved across the floor to look at one of the paintings the floorboards would creak in protest, as if in pain. The atmosphere was one of neglect and deep loneliness. As she lifted each dustsheet off the furniture she got a sense she was uncovering history. What stories could each piece tell? There was a George IV mahogany writing table, a Queen Anne burr-elm chest of drawers, a seventeenth-century Italian walnut side cabinet, a Regency spoon-back chair, as well as a set of four Regency mahogany and brass inlaid chairs, and an Italian gilt wood girandole mirror with embellished surround. How many lives had they watched go by? How many conversations had they overheard?

Along with the furniture, inside some of the cabinets there were Chinese glass snuff bottles, bronze Buddhas, jade Ming dynasty vases and countless ceramics and glassware. So many beautiful treasures locked away where no one could see and enjoy them.

Why was Leandro so intent on getting rid of them? Didn't he have a single sentimental bone in his body? His father had painstakingly collected all of these valuable items. It would have taken him years and years and oodles of money. Why then get rid of them as if they were nothing more than charity shop donations? Surely there was something he would want to keep as a memento?

It didn't make sense.

Miranda went outside for a breath of fresh air after breathing in so much dust. The afternoon was surprisingly warm, but then, this was the French Riviera, she thought. No wonder the English came here in droves for their holidays. Even the light against the old buildings had a certain quality to it—a muted, pastel glow that enhanced the gorgeous architecture.

She took a walk about the garden where weeds ran rampant amongst the spindly arms of roses and underneath the untrimmed hedges. A Virginia creeper was in full autumnal splendour against a stone wall, some of the rich russet and gold leaves crunching and crackling underneath her feet as she walked past.

Miranda caught sight of a small marble statue of an angel through a gap in the unkempt hedge towards the centre of the garden. The hedge had grown so tall it had created a secret hideaway like a maze hiding the Minotaur at the centre of it. The pathway leading to it was littered with leaves and weeds as if no one had been along here for a long time. There was a cobweb-covered wooden bench in the little alcove in front of the statue, providing a secluded spot for quiet reflection. But when she got close she realised it wasn't a statue of an angel after all; it was of a small child of two or three years old.

Miranda bent down to look at the brass plaque that

was all but covered by strangling weeds. She pushed them aside to read:

Rosamund Clemente Allegretti.
Lost but never forgotten.

There was a birth date of thirty years ago but the space where the date of passing should be was blank with just an open-ended dash.

Who was she? Who was this little girl who had been immortalised in white marble?

The sound of a footfall crunching on the leaves behind her made Miranda's heart miss a beat. She scrambled to her feet to see the tall figure of Leandro coming towards her but then, when he saw what was behind her, he stopped dead. It was like he had been struck with something. Blind-sided. Stunned. His features were bleached of colour, going chalk-white beneath his tan. The column of his throat moved up and down: once. Twice. Three times. His eyes twitched, and then flickered, as if in pain.

'You startled me, creeping up on me like that,' Miranda said to fill the eerie silence. 'I thought you were—'

'A ghost?'

Something about his tone made the hair on the back of her neck stand on end. But it was as if he were talking to himself, not her. He seemed hardly even aware she was there. His gaze was focussed on the statue, his brow heavily puckered—even more than usual.

Miranda leaned back against the cool pine-scented

green of the hedge as he moved past her to stand in front of the statue. When he touched the little child's head with one of his hands, she noticed it was visibly shaking.

'Who is she?' she said.

His hand fell away from the child's head to hang by his side. 'My sister.'

She gaped at him in surprise. 'Your *sister*?'

He wasn't looking at her but at the statue, his brows still drawn together in a deep crevasse. 'Rosie. She disappeared when I was six years old. She was three.'

Disappeared? Miranda swallowed so convulsively she felt the walls of her throat close in on each other. *He had a sister who had disappeared?* The shock was like a slap. A punch. A wrecking ball banging against her heart. Why hadn't he said something? For all these years he'd given the impression he was an only child. What a heart-breaking tragedy to keep hidden for all this time. Why hadn't he told his closest friends? 'You never said anything about having a sister. Not once. To anyone.'

'I know,' he said on an expelled breath. 'It was easier than explaining.'

Why hadn't she put two and two together before now? Of course that was why he was so standoffish. Grief did that. It kept you isolated in an invisible bubble of pain. No one could reach you and you couldn't reach out. She knew the process all too well. 'Because it was too…painful?' she said.

He looked at her then, his dark eyes full of silent

suffering. 'It was my way of coping,' he said. 'Talking about her made it worse. It still does.'

'I'm sorry.'

He gave her a sombre movement of his lips before he turned back to look at the statue. He stood there for a long moment, barely a muscle moving on his face apart from an in-and-out movement on his lean cheek, as if he were using every ounce of self-control to keep his emotions in check.

'My father must've had this made,' he said after a long moment. 'I didn't know it existed until now. I just glanced at the garden when I came yesterday—I couldn't see this from the house.'

Miranda bit her lip as she watched him looking at the statue. He had his hands in his pockets and his shoulders were hunched forward slightly. Bone-deep sadness was etched in the landscape of his face.

She silently put a hand on his forearm and gave it a comforting squeeze. He turned his head to look down at her, his eyes meshing with hers as one of his hands came down on top, anchoring hers beneath his. She felt the imprint of his long, strong fingers, the warmth of his palm—the skin-on-skin touch that made something inside her belly shift sideways.

His gaze held hers steady.

Her breathing stalled. Her pulse quickened. Her heartbeat tripped and then raced.

Time froze.

The sounds of the garden—the twittering birds, the breeze ruffling the leaves, the drip of a leaky tap near one of the unkempt beds—faded into the background.

'My father wouldn't allow my mother to pack any-thing away,' Leandro said. 'He couldn't accept Rosie was gone. It was one of the reasons they split up. My mother wanted to move on. He couldn't.'

'And you got caught in the crossfire,' Miranda said.

He dropped his hand from where it was covering hers, stepping away from her as if he needed space to breathe. To think. To regroup. 'I was supposed to be looking after her,' he said after another beat or two of silence. 'The day she disappeared.'

Miranda frowned. 'But you were only what—six? That's not old enough to babysit.'

He gave her one of his hollow looks. 'We were on the beach. I can take you to the exact spot. My mother only walked ten or so metres away to get us an ice-cream. When she came back, Rosie was gone. I didn't hear or see anything. I turned my head to look at a boat that was going past and when I turned back she wasn't there. No one saw anything. It was crowded that hot summer day so no one would've noticed if a child was carried crying from the beach. Not back then.'

Miranda felt a choking lump come to her throat at the agony of what he had been through—the heartache, the distress of not knowing—*never* knowing what had happened to his baby sister. Wondering if she was alive or dead. Wondering if she had suffered. Wondering if there was something—*anything*—he could have done to stop it. How had he endured it?

By blaming himself.

'It wasn't your fault,' she said. 'How can you feel it was your fault? You were only a baby yourself. You shouldn't have been blamed. Your parents were wrong to put that on you.'

'They didn't,' he said. 'Not openly, although my father couldn't help himself in later years.'

So many pennies were beginning to drop. This was why Leandro's father had drunk to senselessness. This was why his mother had moved abroad, remarried, had three children in quick succession and had been always too busy to make time to see him. This was why Leandro had spent so many weekends and school holidays at Ravensdene, because he'd no longer had a home and family to go to. It was unbearably sad to think that all the times Leandro had joined her brothers he had carried this terrible burden. Alone. He hadn't told anyone of the tragedy. Not even his closest friends knew of the gut-wrenching heartache he had been through. And was *still* going through.

'I don't know what to say…' She brushed at her moist eyes with the sleeve of her top. 'It's just so terribly sad. I can't bear the thought of how you've suffered this all alone.'

Leandro reached out and grazed her cheek with a lazy fingertip, his expression rueful. 'I didn't mean to make you cry.'

'I can't help it.' Miranda sniffed and went searching for a tissue but before she could find one up her sleeve he produced the neatly ironed square of a clean white handkerchief. She took it from him with a grateful glance. 'Thanks.'

'My father stubbornly clung to hope,' Leandro said. 'He kept Rosie's room exactly as it was the day she went missing because he'd convinced himself that one day she'd come back. My mother couldn't bear it. She thought it was pathological.'

Miranda scrunched the handkerchief into a ball inside her hand, thinking of the football sweater of Mark's she kept in her wardrobe. Every year on his birthday she would put it on, breathing in the ever-fading scent of him. She kept telling herself it was time to give it back to his parents but she could never quite bring herself to do it. 'Everyone has their own way of grieving,' she said.

'Maybe.'

'Can I see it?'

'Rosie's room?'

'Would you mind?' she said.

He let out a ragged-sounding breath. 'It will have to be packed up sooner or later.'

Miranda walked back to the villa with him. She was deeply conscious of how terribly painful this would be for him. Didn't she feel it every time she visited Mark's parents? They had left his room intact too. Unable to let go of his things because by removing them they would finally have to accept he was gone for ever. But at least Mark's parents were in agreement.

How difficult it must have been for Leandro's mother, trying to move on while his father had been holding back. The loss of a child tested the strongest marriage. Leandro's parents had divorced within two years of Rosie's disappearance. How much had Leandro suffered during that time and since? Estranged from his alcoholic father, shunned by his mother, too busy with her new family.

After the bright light of outdoors the shadows inside the villa seemed all the more ghostly. A chill shimmied down her spine as she climbed the groaning stairs with Leandro.

The room was the third along the corridor—the door she had noticed was locked earlier. Leandro selected a key from a bunch of keys he had in his pocket. The sound of the lock turning over was as sharp and clear as a rifle shot.

Miranda stepped inside, her breath catching in her throat as she took in the little fairy-tale princess bed with its faded pink-and-white cover and the fluffy toys and dolls arranged on the pillow. There was a doll's pram and a beautifully crafted doll's house with gorgeous miniature furniture under the window. There was a child's dressing table with a toy make-up set and a hairbrush lying beside it.

There was a framed photograph hanging on the wall above the bed of a little girl with a mop of dark brown curls, apple-chubby cheeks and a cheeky smile.

Miranda turned to look at Leandro. He was stony faced but she could sense what he was feeling. His grief was palpable. 'Thank you for showing me,' she said. 'It's a beautiful room.'

His throat moved up and down over a swallow. 'She was a great little kid.' He picked up one of the fluffy toys that had fallen forward on the bed—a floppy-eared rabbit—and turned it over in his hands. 'I bought this for her third birthday with my pocket money. She called him Flopsy.'

Miranda blinked a couple of times, surprised her voice worked at all when she finally spoke. 'What will you do with her things once you sell the villa?'

His frown flickered on his forehead. 'I haven't thought that far ahead.'

'You might want to keep some things for when you have your own children,' Miranda said.

She got a sudden vision of him holding a newborn baby, his features softened in tenderness, his large, capable hands cradling the little bundle with care and gentleness. Her heart contracted. He would make a wonderful father. He would be kind and patient. He wouldn't shout and swear and throw tantrums, like her father had done when things hadn't gone his way. Leandro would make a child feel safe and loved and protected. He would be the strong, dependable rock his children would rely on no matter what life dished up.

He put the rabbit back down on the bed as if it had bitten him. 'I'll donate it all to charity.'

'But don't you—?'

'No.'

The implacability of his tone made her stomach feel strangely hollow. 'Don't you want to get married and have a family one day?'

His eyes collided with hers. 'Do you?'

Miranda shifted her gaze and rolled her lips together for a moment. 'We're not talking about me.'

The line of his mouth was tight. White. 'Maybe we should.'

She pulled back her shoulders. Lifted her chin. Held his steely look even though it made the backs of her knees feel fizzy. 'It's different for me.'

A glimmer of cynicism lit his dark gaze. 'Why's that?'

'I made a promise.'

Leandro gave a short mocking laugh. 'To a dying man—*a boy*?'

Miranda gritted her teeth. How many times did she have to have this conversation? 'We *loved* each other.'

'You loved the idea of love,' he said. 'He was your first boyfriend—the first person to show an interest in you. It's my bet if he hadn't got sick he would've moved on within a month or two. He used your sweet, compliant nature to—'

'That's not true!'

'He didn't want to die alone and lonely,' he went on with a callous disregard for her feelings. 'He tied you to him, making you promise stuff no one in their right mind would promise. Not at that age.'

Miranda put her hand up to her ears in a childish attempt to block the sound of his taunting voice. 'No! *No!*'

'You were a kid,' he said. 'A romantically dazed kid who couldn't see how she was being used towards the end. He had cancer—the big, disgusting C-word. In an instant he had gone from being one of the top jocks to one of the untouchables. But he knew *you* wouldn't let him down. Not the sweet, loyal little Miranda Ravensdale who was looking for a Shakespearean tragedy to pin her name on.'

'You're wrong,' she said. 'Wrong. Wrong. *Wrong.* You have no right to say such things to me. You don't understand what we had. *You* don't commit to a relationship longer than a few weeks. What would you know of loyalty and commitment? Mark and I were friends for years—*years*—before we became...more intimate.'

He tugged her hands down and loosely gripped her wrists in his hands so she could feel every one of his fingers burning against her flesh. 'Am I wrong?' he asked. 'Am I really?'

Miranda pulled out of his hold with an almighty wrench that made her stumble backwards. How dared he mock her? How dared he make fun of her? How *dared* he question her love and commitment for Mark and his for her? 'You have no right to question my relationship with Mark. No right at all. I loved him. I loved him and I *still* love him. Nothing you can say or do will ever change that.'

His mouth slanted in a cynical half-smile. 'I could change that. I know I could. All it would take is one little kiss.'

Miranda coughed out a laugh but even to her ears it sounded unconvincing. 'Like *that's* ever going to happen.'

He was suddenly close. Way too close. His broad fingertip was suddenly on the underside of her chin without her knowing how it got there. All she registered was the warm, branding feeling of it resting there, holding her captive with the mesmerising force of his bottomless dark gaze.

'Is that a dare, Sleeping Beauty?' he said in a silky tone.

Miranda felt his words slither down her spine like an unfurling satin ribbon running away from its spool. Her knees threatened to give way. Her belly quivered with a host of needs she couldn't even name. She couldn't tear her eyes away from his coal-black gaze. It was drawing her in like a magnet does a tiny iron filing.

She became aware of her breasts inside the lacy cups of her bra. They prickled and swelled as if stimulated to attention by the deep, burry sound of his voice. The below-the-ocean-floor, rumbly bass of his voice—the voice that did strange things to her feminine body.

Her inner core clenched in a contraction of raw, primal need. Her blood ticked, raced, through the network of her veins at breakneck frenzied speed. Every pore of her body ached for his touch, for the sensuous glide of his fingers, for the hot sweep of his tongue, for the stabbing thrust of his body.

But finally a vestige of pride came to her rescue.

Miranda dipped out from under his fingertip and rubbed at her chin as she sent him a warning glare. 'Don't play games with me, Leandro.'

A sardonic gleam shone in his dark eyes. 'You think I was joking?'

She didn't know what to think. Not when he looked at her like that—with smouldering black-as-pitch eyes that seemed to see right through her defences. That sensually contoured mouth shouldn't tempt her. She shouldn't be wondering what it would feel like against her own. She shouldn't be looking at his mouth as if she had no control over her gaze.

He was her brothers' friend. He was practically one

of the family. He had seen her with pimples and braces. He had seen her lying on the sofa with a hot-water bottle pressed to her cramping belly. He could have any girl he wanted. Why would he want to kiss her unless it was to score points? He thought her loyalty to Mark was ridiculous. How better to prove it by having her go weak-kneed when he kissed her?

Not. Going. To. Happen.

She bent her head and made to go past him. 'I'm going to do something about dinner.'

He caught her left arm on the way past, his fingers forming a loose bracelet around her wrist. His gaze drew hers to his with an unspoken command. She couldn't have looked away if she tried. Her breath caught as his thumb found her pulse. The warmth of his fingers made her spine fizz and her knees tremble. 'There's no food in the house,' he said. 'I haven't had time to shop. Let's go out.'

Miranda chewed the inside of her lip. 'I'm not sure that's such a good idea…'

His thumb stroked the underside of her wrist in slow motion. 'Just dinner,' he said. 'Don't worry. I won't try any moves on you. Your brothers would skin me alive if I did.'

The thought of him making a move on her made the hot spill in her belly spread through her pelvis and down between her thighs like warmed treacle. It was hard enough controlling her reaction to him as he stroked her wrist in that tantalising manner. Her senses went into a tailspin with every mesmerising movement of his fingers against her skin. What would it do to her to feel his mouth on hers? To feel his molten touch on her breasts and her other aching intimate places?

But then, she thought: *what had her brothers to do with anything?* If she wanted to get involved with Leandro—if things had been different, that was—then that would be up to her, not to Julius and Jake to give the go ahead. 'I'm hardly your type in any case,' Miranda said, carefully extricating her wrist from his fingers.

His expression was now inscrutable. 'Does that bother you?'

Did it?

Of course it did. Men like Leandro didn't notice girls like her. She was the type of girl who was invisible to most men. She was too girl-next-door. Shy and reserved, not vivacious and outgoing. Pretty but not stunning. Petite, not voluptuous. If it hadn't been for his friendship with her brothers he probably wouldn't have given her the time of day. She wasn't just a wallflower. She was wallpaper. Bland, boring, beige wallpaper.

'Not at all,' Miranda said, rubbing at her still-tingling wrist. 'You've a perfect right to date whomever you chose.'

But please don't do it while I'm under the same roof.

CHAPTER FOUR

LEANDRO WAITED AT the foot of the stairs for Miranda. He had showered and changed and tried not to think about how close he had been to kissing her earlier. He had always kept his distance in the past. It wasn't that he hadn't noticed her. He had. He was always viscerally aware of how close she was to him. It was like picking up a radar frequency inside his body. If she was within touching distance, his body was acutely aware of her every movement. Even if it was as insignificant as her lifting one of her hands to her face to tuck back a stray strand of hair. He felt it in his body.

If she so much as walked past him every cell in his body stood to attention. If she sent her tongue out over her beautiful mouth he felt as if she had stroked it over him intimately. When she smiled that hesitant, shy, nervous smile every pore of his skin contracted with primal need as he imagined her losing that shyness with him. As soon as he caught a trace of her scent he would feel a rush through his flesh. His blood would bloom with such heat he could feel it charging through his pelvis and down his legs.

But he kept his distance.

Always.

She was the kid sister of his two closest friends. It was an unspoken code between mates: no poaching of sisters. If things didn't work out, it would strain everyone's relationship. He had seen enough with the angst between Jake and Jasmine. The air could be cut with a knife when those two were in the same room. The fallout from their fiery spat still made everyone uncomfortable even seven years after the event. You couldn't mention Jaz's name around Jake without his expression turning to thunder. And Jaz turned into a hissing and spitting wildcat if Jake so much as glanced her way.

Leandro wasn't going to add to the mix with a dalliance with Miranda, even if she did somehow manage to move on from the loss of her teenage boyfriend. She wasn't the type to settle for a casual fling. She was way too old-fashioned and conservative for that. She would want the fairy tale: the house with the picket fence and cottage flowers, the kids and the dog.

He wondered if she had even had proper sex with her boyfriend. They had started officially dating when she'd been fourteen, which in his opinion was a little young. He knew teenagers had sex younger than ever but had she been ready emotionally? Why was she so determined to cling to a promise that essentially locked her up for life? He didn't understand why she would do such a thing. How could she possibly think she'd loved Mark enough to make that sort of sacrifice?

He had always had the feeling Mark Redbank had clung to Miranda for all the wrong reasons. She be-

lieved it to have been true love but Leandro wasn't
so sure. Call him cynical, but he'd always suspected
Mark had used Miranda, especially towards the end.
He thought Mark had played up his feelings for her
to keep her tied to him. The decent thing would have
been to set her free but apparently Mark had extracted
a death-bed promise with her that she was stubbornly
determined to stick to.

But touching her had awakened something in Leandro. He had never touched her before. Not even when
he came to visit the family at Ravensdene. He had always avoided the kiss on the cheek to say hello, mostly
because she was too shy to offer it and he would never
make the first move. He had never even shaken her
hand. He had made every effort to avoid physical contact. He knew she saw him as a cold fish, aloof, distant.
He had been happy to keep it that way.

But being in that room with all those memories and
all that crushing grief had pushed him off-balance.
Something had been unleashed inside him. Something
he wasn't sure he could control. Now he had touched
Miranda he wanted to touch her again. It was an urge
that pulsed through him. The feel of her creamy skin
beneath his palm, against his fingers, her silky hair
tickling the back of his hand, had stirred his blood
until it roared through his body like an out of control
freight train. It made him think forbidden thoughts.
Thoughts he had never allowed himself to think before now. Thoughts of her lying pinned by his body, his
need pumping into her as her cries of pleasure filled
the air.

The brief flare of temper she had shown confirmed everything he had suspected about her. Underneath her ice-maiden façade was a passionate young woman just crying out for physical expression. He could see it in the way she held herself together so primly, as if she was frightened of breaking free from the tight moral restraints she had placed around herself. Kissing her would have proven it. He wanted to taste that soft, innocent bow of a mouth and feel her shudder all over with longing. To thrust his tongue between those beautiful lips and taste the sweet, moist heat of her mouth. To have her tongue tangle with his in a sexy coupling that was a prelude to smoking-hot sex.

He clenched his hands into tight fists as he wrestled with his conscience. He wasn't in a good place right now. He was acting totally out of character. It would be wrong to try it on with her. He could slake his lust the way he usually did—with someone who knew the game and was happy with his rules. He didn't do long term. The longest he did was a month or two—any longer than that and women got ideas of bended knees, rings and promises he couldn't deliver on.

It wasn't that he was against marriage. He believed in it as an institution and admired people who made it work. He even believed it *could* work. He believed it was a good framework in which to bring up children and travel through the cycles and seasons of life with someone who had the same vision and values. He was quietly envious of Julius's relationship with Holly Perez. But he didn't allow himself to think too long about how it would be to have a life partner to build a future with—to have someone to hope and dream with.

He was used to living on his own.

He preferred it. He didn't have to make idle conversation. He didn't have to meet someone else's emotional needs. He could get on with his work any hour of the day—particularly when he couldn't sleep—and no one would question him.

Leandro heard a soft footfall at the top of the stairs and looked up to see Miranda gliding down like a graceful swan. She was wearing a knee-length milky-coffee-coloured dress with a cashmere pashmina around her slim shoulders. It would have been a nondescript colour on someone else but with her porcelain skin and auburn hair it was perfect. She had scooped her hair up into a makeshift but stylish knot at the back of her head, which highlighted the elegant length of her slim neck. She was wearing a string of pearls and pearl studs in her earlobes that showcased the creamy, smooth perfection of her skin and, as she got closer, he could pick up the fresh, flowery scent of her perfume. Her brown eyes were made up with subtle shades of eye shadow and her fan-like lashes had been lengthened and thickened with mascara.

Her mouth—*dear God in heaven, why couldn't he stop looking at her mouth?*—was shiny with a strawberry-coloured lip gloss.

A light blush rode along her cheekbones as she came to stand before him. 'I'm sorry for keeping you waiting…'

Leandro felt her perfume ambush his senses; the

freesia notes were fresh and light but there was a hint of something a little more complex under the surface. It teased his nostrils, toyed with his imagination, tormented him with its veiled sensual promise. He glanced at her shoes. 'Can you walk in those?'

'Yes.'

'The restaurant is only a few blocks from here,' he said. 'But I can drive if you'd prefer.'

'No, a walk would be lovely,' she said.

They walked to a French restaurant Leandro informed Miranda he had found the day before. Every step of the walk, she was aware of the distance between them. It never varied. It was as if he had calculated what would be appropriate and rigorously stuck to it. He walked on the road side of the footpath just like the well-bred gentleman she knew him to be. He took care at the intersections they came to making sure it was safe to cross against the traffic and other pedestrians.

Miranda was aware of him there beside her. Even though he didn't touch her, not even accidently to brush against her, she could feel his male presence. It made her skin lift, tighten and tingle. It made her body feel strangely excited, as if something caged inside her belly was holding its breath, eagerly anticipating the brush of his flesh against hers.

Miranda realised then she had never been on a proper dinner date with an adult man. When she and Mark went out they had done teenage things—walks and café chats, trips to the cinema and fast-food outlets and the occasional friend's party. But then he had been diagnosed and their dates had been in the hospital or, on rare occasions when he'd been feeling well enough, in the hospital cafeteria. They had never gone out to dinner in a proper restaurant. They had never gone clubbing. They had never even gone out for a drink as they had been under age.

How weird to be doing it first with Leandro, she thought. It made her feel as if something had shifted in their relationship. A subtle change that put them on a different platform. He was no longer her brothers' close friend but her first proper adult dinner-date. But of course they weren't actually dating, no matter what Jaz thought about the way he looked at her. Jaz was probably imagining it. Why would Leandro be interested in her? She was too shy. Too ordinary. Too beige.

The small intimate restaurant was tucked in one of the cobbled side streets and it had both inside and outside dining. When Leandro asked her for her preference, Miranda chose to sit outside, as the October evening was beautifully mild, but also because after the dusty, brooding, shadowy interior of his father's villa she thought it would be nice to have some fresh air. For Leandro, as well as her.

The weight of grief in that sad old villa had been hard enough for her to deal with, let alone him. It pained her to think he carried the burden of guilt— guilt that should never have been laid on his young child's shoulders. She couldn't stop thinking of him as a six-year-old boy—quiet, sensitive, intelligent, caring. How could his parents have put that awful yoke upon his young shoulders?

It was a terrible tragedy that his sister Rosie had gone missing. A heart-breaking, gut-wrenching tragedy that could not be resolved in any way now that would be healing. But his parents had been the adults. They'd been the ones with the responsibility to keep their children safe. It hadn't been Leandro's responsibility. Children could not be held accountable for doing what only an adult should do. Children as young as six were not reliable babysitters. Not even for two or three minutes. They were at the mercy of their immature impulses. It wasn't fair to blame them for what was typical of that stage of childhood development. It wasn't right to punish a child for simply being a child.

How much had Leandro suffered with that terrible burden? He had shouldered it on his own for all this time—twenty-seven years. He had stored it away deep inside him—unable to connect properly with people because of it. He always stood at the perimeter of social gatherings. He was set apart by the tragic secret he carried. He hadn't even told her brothers about Rosie and yet he had asked Miranda to come here and help him with his father's collection. What did *that* mean? Had it been an impulsive thing on his part? She had never thought of him as an impulsive man. He measured everything before he acted. He thought before he spoke. He considered things from every angle.

Why *had* he asked her?

Was it a subconscious desire on his part to connect? What sort of connection was he after? Could Jaz be right? Could he be after a more intimate connection? Was that why he was challenging her over her com-

mitment to Mark? Making her face her convictions in
the face of temptation—a temptation she had never felt
quite like this before?

He thought her silly for staying true to her commitment to Mark. But then Leandro wasn't known for
longevity in relationships. He wasn't quite the one-
night-stand man her brother Jake was but she hadn't
heard of any relationship of Leandro's lasting longer
than a month or two. He moved around with work a
lot which would make it difficult for him to settle.
But even so she didn't see him as the guy with a girl
in every port.

Would Miranda's time here with him help him to
move past the tragedy of Rosie? Would he feel freer
once his father's things were packed up and sold? Once
all this sadness was put away for good?

Once they were seated at their table with drinks in
front of them Miranda took a covert look at him while
he perused the menu. The sad memories from being
in his little sister's room were etched on his face. His
dark-chocolate eyes looked tired and drawn, the two
lines running either side of his mouth seemed deeper
and his ever-present frown more firmly entrenched.

He looked up and his eyes meshed with hers, making something in her stomach trip like a foot missing
a step. 'Have you decided?' he said.

Miranda had to work hard not to stare at his mouth.
He had showered and shaved, yet the persistent stubble
was evident along his jaw and around his well-shaped
mouth. She had to curl her fingers into her palms to
stop herself from reaching across the table to touch the

peppered lean and tanned skin, to trace the sculptured line of his beautiful mouth. His thick hair was cut in a short no-nonsense style, although she could see a light sheen amongst the deep grooves where he had used some sort of hair product. Even with the distance of the table between them she could smell the hint of citrus and wood in his aftershave.

'Um…' She looked back at the menu, chewing on her lower lip. 'I think I'll have the *coq au vin*. You?'

He closed the menu with a definitive movement. 'Same.'

Miranda took a tentative sip of her white wine. He had ordered one as well but he had so far not touched it. Did he avoid alcohol because of his father's problems with it? Or was it just a part of his careful, keeping-control-at-all-times personality?

Self-discipline was something she admired in a man. Her father had always lacked it, which was more than obvious, given this latest debacle over his love child. But Leandro wasn't the sort of man to be driven by impulse. He was responsible, mature and sensible. He was the sort of man people came to for help and advice. He was reliable and principled. Which made what had happened to him all the more tragic. How hard it must be for him to come back here to the place where it all began. His life had changed for ever. He carried that burden of guilt. It had defined him. Shaped him. And yet he had kept it to himself for all those years.

'If I hadn't found Rosie's statue in the garden would you have told me about her?' Miranda said into the little silence.

His fingers toyed with the stem of his glass. 'I was planning to. Eventually.'

She watched as his frown pulled heavily at his brow. 'Leandro... I really want to say how much I feel for you. For what you're going through. For what you've been through. I feel I'm only just coming to understand you after knowing you for all these years.'

He gave her a ghost of a smile. It was not much more than a flicker across his lips but it warmed her heart, as if someone had shone a beam of light through a dark crack. 'I was a little hard on you earlier,' he said.

'It's okay,' Miranda said. 'I get it from my brothers and Jaz too. And my parents.'

'It's only because they love you,' he said. 'They want you to be happy.'

Miranda put her glass down, her fingers tracing the gentle slope on the circular base. 'I know...but it wasn't just Mark I loved. His family—his parents—are the loveliest people. They always made me feel so special. So included.'

'Do you still see them?'

'Yes.'

'Is that wise?'

Miranda frowned as she met his unwavering gaze. 'Why wouldn't I visit them? They're the family I wish I'd had.'

'It might not be helping them to move on.'

'What about your mother?' she said, deftly changing the subject. 'Does she want you to be happy?'

He gave a nonchalant shrug but his mouth had taken

on that grim look she always associated with him. 'On some level, maybe.'

'Do you ever see her?'

'Occasionally.'

'When was the last time?' Miranda asked.

He turned the base of his glass around with an exacting, precise movement like he was turning a combination lock on a safe. 'I went down for one of my half-brother's birthdays a couple of months ago.'

'And?'

He looked at her again. 'It was okay.'

Miranda cocked her head at him. 'Just okay?'

He gave her a rueful grimace. 'It was Cameron who invited me. I wouldn't have gone if he hadn't wanted me to be there. I didn't stay long.'

Miranda wondered what sort of reception he'd got from his mother. Had she greeted him warmly or coldly? Had she tolerated him being there or embraced his presence? How did his mother's husband treat him? Did he accept him as one of the family or make him feel like an outsider who could never belong? There were so many questions she wanted to ask. Things she wanted to know about him, but she didn't want to bombard him. It would take time to peel back the layers to his personality. He was so deeply private and going too hard too soon would very likely cause him to clam up. 'How old are your half-brothers?'

'Cam is twenty-eight, Alistair twenty-seven and Hugh is twenty-six.' He turned his glass another notch. 'My mother would have had more children but it wasn't to be.'

'Three boys in quick succession…' she murmured, thinking out loud.

'But no girl, which was what she really wanted.'

Miranda saw the flash of pain pass over his features. 'I'm not sure having any amount of children would make up for the one she lost. But in a way she lost two children, didn't she?'

Leandro's mouth tilted cynically. 'Don't feel sorry for me, *ma petite*,' he said. 'I'm a big boy.'

Hearing him switch to French from Italian endearments was enough to set her pulse racing all over again. His voice was so deep and mellifluous she could have listened to him read a boring financial report and still her heart would race. 'It seems to me you've always had to be a big boy,' Miranda said. 'You've spent so much of your childhood and adolescence alone.'

'I had your family to go to.'

'Yes, but it wasn't *your* family,' she said. 'You must have felt that keenly at times.'

He picked up his wine glass and examined the contents, as if it were a vintage wine he wanted to savour. But then he put it back down again. 'I owe a lot to your family,' he said. 'In particular to your brothers. We had some good times down at Ravensdene. Some really great times.'

'And yet you never once mentioned Rosie to them.'

'I thought about it a couple of times… Many times, actually.' He fingered the base of his glass again. 'But in the end it was easier keeping that part of my life separate. Except, of course, when my father came to town.'

'You were worried he would blurt something in his drunken state?' Miranda said.

He gave her a world-weary look. 'Anyone being drunk is not a pretty sight but my father took it to a whole new level. He always liked a drink but I don't ever remember seeing him flat-out drunk as a child. Losing Rosie tipped him over. He numbed himself with alcohol in order to cope.'

'Did he ever try and get help for his drinking?'

'I offered to pay for rehab numerous times but he wouldn't hear of it,' Leandro said. 'He said he didn't have a problem. He was able to control it. Mostly he did. But not when he was with me, especially in latter years.'

Miranda's heart clenched. How painful it must have been for him to witness the devastation of his father's life while being cognisant that *he* was deemed responsible for it. It was too cruel. Too sad. Too unbearable to think of someone as decent, sensitive and wonderful as Leandro being tortured so. 'It must have been awful to watch him slide into such self-destruction and not be able to do anything to help,' she said. 'But you mustn't blame yourself, Leandro. Not now. Not after all this time. Your father made choices. He could've got help at any point. You did what you could. You can't force someone to get help. They have to be willing to accept there's a problem in the first place.'

He looked back at the glass of untouched wine in front of him, his brows drawn together in a tightly knitted frown. Miranda put her hand out and covered his where it was resting on the snowy-white tablecloth.

He looked up and met her gaze with the dark intensity of his. 'You're a nice kid, Miranda,' he said in a gruff burr that made the base of her spine shiver.

A nice kid.

Didn't he see her as anything other than the kid sister of his best mates? And why did it bother her if he didn't see she was a fully grown woman? It shouldn't bother her at all. She wasn't going to break her promise to Mark. She couldn't. For the last seven years she had stayed true to her commitment. She took pride in being so steadfast, so strong and so loyal, especially in this day and age when people slept with virtual strangers.

Her words were the last words Mark had heard before he'd left this world. How could she retract them?

A promise was a promise.

Miranda lowered her gaze and pulled back her hand but even when it was back in her lap she could feel the warmth of Leandro's skin against her palm.

The rest of the meal continued with the conversation on much lighter ground. He asked her about her work at the gallery and, an hour and two courses later, she realised he had cleverly drawn her out without revealing anything of his own work and the stresses and demands it placed on him.

'Enough about me,' she said, pushing her wine glass away. 'Tell me about your work. What made you go into forensic accounting?'

'I was always good at maths,' he said. 'But straight accounting wasn't enough for me. I was drawn to the challenge of uncovering complicated financial systems. It's a bit like breaking a code. I find it satisfying.'

'And clearly financially rewarding,' Miranda said.

He gave a slight movement of his lips that might have been considered a smile. 'I do okay.'

He was being overly modest, Miranda thought. He didn't brandish his wealth as some people did. There were no private jets, Italian sports cars and luxurious holidays all over the globe; he had invested his money wisely in property and shares and gave a considerable amount to charity. Not that he made that public. She had only heard about it via her brother Julius, who was also known for his philanthropy.

Just as they were leaving the restaurant, once Leandro had paid the bill, a party of people came towards them from down the lane. Miranda wouldn't have taken much notice except a woman of about thirty or so peeled away from the group to approach Leandro.

'Leandro?' she said. 'Fancy running into you here! I haven't heard from you for a while. I've come over for a wedding of a friend. Are you here on business?'

'How are you?'

Leandro gave the young woman a kiss on both cheeks. 'Fine. You?'

The woman eyed Miranda. 'Aren't you going to introduce us?' she asked Leandro with a glinting look.

'Miranda, this is Nicole Holmes,' he said. 'We worked for the same accounting firm before I left to go out on my own. Nicole, this is Miranda Ravensdale.'

Nicole's perfectly shaped brows lifted. 'As in *the* infamous Ravensdales?' she said.

Miranda gave a tight smile. 'Pleased to meet you, Nicole.'

Nicole's gaze travelled over Miranda in an assessing, sizing-up manner common to some women when they encountered someone they presumed was competition. 'I've been reading all about your father's secret love-child in the papers and gossip mags,' she said. 'Have you met your new sister yet?'

Miranda felt the muscles in her spine tighten like concrete. 'Not yet.'

Nicole glanced at Leandro. 'So are you two…?' She left the sentence hanging suggestively.

'No,' Leandro said. 'We're old friends.'

Miranda knew it was silly of her to be feeling piqued that he hadn't made their relationship sound a little more exciting. But the woman was clearly an old flame of his, by the way she kept giving him the eye. Why couldn't he have pretended they were seeing each other? Or was he hoping for a little for-old-times'-sake tryst with Nicole? The thought of Leandro bringing someone like Nicole back to the villa made Miranda's stomach churn. Nothing against Nicole, but surely he could do better than that? Nicole seemed… hard—too streetwise to be sensitive. But maybe that was all he wanted, Miranda thought. Sex without sensitivity. Without strings. Without attachment.

'So what are you doing in Nice?' Nicole said.

'I'm seeing to some family business,' Leandro said.

Nicole's green eyes met Miranda's. 'And you're helping him?'

'Erm…yes,' Miranda said.

Nicole turned her cat's gaze back on to Leandro. 'How about we meet for a drink while you're here?'

she said. 'I'm here another couple of days. Name the time and the place. I'm pretty flexible.'

I just bet you are, Miranda thought with a savage twist of jealousy deep in her gut.

'I'll give you a call tomorrow,' Leandro said. 'Where are you staying?'

'At Le Negresco.' Nicole lifted her hand in a girlish fingertip wave as she backed away to join her friends who were waiting for her at the end of the lane. 'I'll be seeing you.'

Miranda waited until Nicole and her cronies had disappeared before she turned to Leandro with a look of undiluted disgust. *'Really?'* she said.

He looked down at her with his customary frown. 'What's wrong?'

She blew out a breath. 'I swear to God I will *never* understand men. What do you see in her? No, don't answer that. I saw the size of her breasts. Are they real? And is she really blonde or did it come out of a bottle?'

Leandro's frown softened. 'You're jealous.'

Miranda cast him a haughty glare. 'Jealous? Seriously? Is that what you think?'

'She's just someone I hang out with occasionally.'

'Oh, I understand,' she said with icy disdain. 'A friend with benefits.'

'You disapprove?'

Miranda didn't want to sound like a Sunday school teacher from the last century but the thought of him hooking up with Nicole made her insides twist into painful knots. 'It's none of my business what you do. I'd just appreciate it if you'd spare me the indignity of having to hear your seduction routine while I'm under the same roof.'

His expression didn't change. He could have been sitting at a poker tournament but she still got the feeling he was amused by her reaction. 'Don't worry,' he said. 'I never bring women like Nicole home. That's what hotels are for.'

Miranda swung away. 'I don't want to hear about it.'

He walked alongside her. 'Do you lecture Jake like this?' he said after they had gone a few paces.

'No, because Jake isn't like you,' she said. 'You're different. You have class—or so I thought.'

'I'm sorry for being such a bitter disappointment.'

Miranda flashed him a glare. 'Will you *stop* it?'

His look was guileless. 'Stop what?'

'You're laughing at me. I know you are.'

He reached out and gently tucked an escaping tendril of her hair back behind her ear. 'It's just sex, *ma petite*. No one is hurting anyone.'

Miranda's breath caught in her throat. His fingers had left the skin at the back of her ear tingling. Was he as tender with a casual lover? Did he touch that woman Nicole as if she were a precious piece of porcelain? Or was it wham, bam, thank you, mam? 'How long have you been—' she put her fingers up in air quotes '—seeing her?'

'A year or two.'

A year or two? Did that mean he was serious about her? Miranda had always got the impression he was a casual dater. But if he'd been seeing Nicole for that long surely it must mean he was serious about her? Was he in love with her? He hadn't looked like a man in love. He had kissed Nicole in a perfunctory way, and on the cheeks, not on the lips. He hadn't even hugged her. 'That seems a long time to be seeing someone,' she said. 'Does that mean you're thinking of—?'

'No,' he said. 'It's not that sort of relationship.'

'What if she falls in love with you?' Miranda said. 'What then?'

'Nicole knows the rules.'

'How often do you see her?' Miranda didn't really want to know. 'Weekly? Monthly?'

'When it's convenient.'

She could feel her lip curling and her insides tightening as if an invisible hand was gripping her intestines. 'So, how often is it convenient? Once a week? Twice a month? Every couple of months?'

'I don't keep a tally, if that's what you're asking,' he said. 'It's not an exclusive relationship.'

Miranda couldn't believe he was living his life in such a shallow manner. He was worth far more than a quick phone call to hook up. Didn't he realise how much he was short-changing himself? Didn't he want more for his life? More emotional intimacy? A deeper connection other than the physical? A casual fling every now and again might have been fine while he was young, but what about as he got older? He was thirty-three years old. Did he really want to spend the rest of his life alone? What about the women he dated? Didn't *they* want more? How could they not want more when he embodied everything most women wanted?

'Don't you have any idea of how *attractive* you are to women?' Miranda said.

His dark eyes were unreadable. 'Am I attractive to you?'

She took a hitching breath, not quite able to hold his gaze. 'I—I don't think of you that way. You're like… like a brother to me.'

He brought her chin up so she had to meet his gaze. 'I'm not feeling like a brother right now. And I have a feeling you're not feeling anything like a sister.'

Miranda swallowed. Was she *that* transparent? Could he see how much of a struggle it was to keep her gaze away from the temptation of his mouth? Could he sense how hard it was keeping her commitment to Mark secure when he looked at her like that? With that smouldering gaze burning through every layer of her resolve like a blowtorch on glacial ice? She sent her tongue out to moisten her sandstone-dry lips and saw his gaze hone in on its passage, as if pulled by a magnet.

She watched spellbound as his mouth lowered towards hers as if in slow motion. There was plenty of time for her to draw back, plenty of time to put some distance between them, but somehow she couldn't get the message through to her addled brain.

She gave a breathless, almost soundless sigh as his lips touched hers. A touch down as soft as fairy feet sent a hot wave of need through her entire body until she felt a shudder go through her from head to toe and back again. She made another helpless noise at the back of her throat as she wound her arms up around his neck, pressing closer, pressing to get more of his firm mouth before it got too far away.

His lips came down harder this time, moving over hers in a possessive manner that made her knees weaken and her spine buckle. His tongue stroked the seam of her mouth, commanding she open to him, and with another little gasp she welcomed him inside. He came in search of her tongue, exploring every corner of her mouth with shockingly intimate, breath-taking expertise. She felt the scrape of his stubble against her chin as he shifted position. Felt the potent stirring of his body against her belly. Felt her own blood racing as desire swept through her like a runaway fire.

Miranda had felt desire as a teenager but it had been nothing like this. That had been a trickle. This was a flood. A tidal wave. A tsunami. This was adult desire. A rampant, clawing need that refused to be assuaged with anything but full possession. She could feel the urgent pleas of her body: the restless ache deep in her core, the tingling of her breasts where they were pressed up hard against his chest.

Kissing in a dark lane wasn't enough. No way was it enough. She wanted to put her hands on his flesh—his gloriously adult, male *healthy* flesh—to feel his body moving over hers with passionate intent. To feel him deep inside her where she ached the most.

But suddenly he pulled away from her.

Miranda felt momentarily off-balance without his arms and body to support her. What was she doing, kissing him like some sex-starved desperado? Her whole body was shaking with the rush of pleasure his mouth had evoked—hot sparks of pleasure that re-verberated in the lower regions of her body. Pulsing, throbbing sparks of forbidden, traitorous pleasure. How could she have let it happen? *Why* had she let it happen? But, rather than show how undone she was, she took refuge in defensive pride. 'Happy now?' she said. 'Proved your point?'

He stood a couple of feet away, one of his hands pushing back through the thick pelt of his hair. It should have come as some small compensation to her that he looked as shell-shocked as she felt but somehow it didn't.

Had he found kissing her distasteful? Unexciting? Not quite up to standard? A host of insecurities flooded through her, leaving a storm of hot colour pooling in her cheeks.

She hadn't kissed anyone but Mark. He had been her first and her last. Their kisses had been nice. Clumsy at first, but then nice. The sex…well, it had seemed to be okay for Mark, but she had found it hard to get her needs met. They'd both been each other's first lover so his inexperience and her shyness hadn't exactly helped.

Then the chemotherapy had made things especially awkward. She hadn't always cared for the smell of Mark's breath or the fact that he was ill most of the time. It had made her feel guilty, being so missish. After Mark's diagnosis she had shied away from shar-ing her body with him because in her youthful igno-rance she had thought she might catch cancer. She had compensated in other ways, pleasuring him manually when he felt up to it. Her guilt over feeling like that had compounded—solidified—her decision to remain loyal to him.

But such inexperience left her stranded when it came to dealing with a man as experienced as Leandro. He was used to women who played the game. Used to hooking up for the sake of convenience before moving on. He wouldn't want the complication of tangling with a technical virgin. Had he sensed her inexperience? Had she somehow communicated it with her response to his kiss?

Leandro let out a long, slow breath as if recalibrating himself. 'That was probably not such a great idea on my part.'

Miranda pulled at her lip with her teeth. 'Was I that bad?'

His brows drew closer together. 'No, of course not. How could you think that?'

She gave a one-shoulder shrug. 'I've only kissed one person before. I'm out of practice.'

He studied her for a long moment. 'Do you miss it?'

'Miss what?'

'Kissing, touching, sex—being with someone.'

Miranda resumed walking and he fell into step beside her at a polite arm's length distance. 'I don't think about it. I made a promise and as far as I'm concerned that's the end of it.'

It wasn't the end of it, Miranda thought as she got into bed half an hour later with her body still madly craving the touch and heat of his. She put her fingers to her mouth, touching where his warm lips had moved so expertly against hers. Her mouth felt different somehow. Softer, fuller, awakened to needs she had ignored for so long.

Needs she would continue to ignore even if it took every ounce of will power she possessed.

CHAPTER FIVE

LEANDRO SPENT AN hour or two over some accounts and files he'd brought with him but he couldn't concentrate. He closed the laptop and got to his feet. Miranda had gone to bed hours ago and everything that was male in him had wanted to join her. He shouldn't have kissed her. He still didn't know why he had. He had been so determined to keep his distance and then it had just… happened. He had been the one to make the first move. He hadn't been able to stop himself from leaning down to the lure of her beautiful, soft, inviting mouth. The taste of her, so sweet, warm and giving, had shaken him. Rocked him. Unsettled him.

Miranda had seemed upset at his on-off relationship with Nicole. But that didn't mean he had the right to kiss her. She was just being protective in a sisterly sort of way.

Sisterly? There was nothing sisterly about the way Miranda had kissed him back. He had felt every tremble in her body as she'd leaned into him. Her gorgeous mouth had given back as good as he had served. The tangled heat of their tongues had made his body respond like a hormone-driven teenager. Since when did he lose control like that? What was he doing even *thinking* about doing more than kissing her?

Leandro stood at the window of the study and looked out at the neglected garden. The moon illuminated the overgrown shapes of the hedges, giving them a grotesque appearance. He couldn't see Rosie's statue from here but knowing it was there made the weight of his grief feel like an anchor hanging off his heart.

Would it *never* ease? This awful sense of guilt that plagued him day and night?

Would packing up Rosie's room bring closure or would it make things even worse? Handling the toys she had played with, touching the clothes she had worn, packing them off to where? Charity? For some stranger to use or to throw out when they were finished with them?

Leandro couldn't keep her things. Why would he? He would have no use for them and he didn't want to turn into another version of his father, making a shrine that in no way would help to heal the past.

It was time to move on.

He opened the door to Rosie's room and stood there for a moment. For the two years after Rosie's disappearance he had come to her room during the night. *Every* night. He had stood in exactly this spot in the doorway, hoping, praying, he would find her neat little shape in the princess bed. That he would see one of her starfish hands resting on the pillow near her little angel face with its halo of dark hair. That he would hear the soft snuffle of her breathing and see the rise and fall of her chest.

He remembered the last time he had stood here. The night before he had been taken to England to live with his mother. He had stood in this doorway with a tsunami of emotion trapped in his chest.

Something in him had died along with Rosie. He could feel the place where it had been. It was a hollow space inside him where hope used to be.

The moon shone a beam over the empty bed where Flopsy the rabbit had slumped forward from his propped up position against the pillows. Leandro moved across the carpet and gently straightened the toy so he was back between the pink elephant and the teddy bear.

He turned from the bed, his heart all but stopping when he saw a small figure framed in the doorway. He blinked and then realised it was Miranda, dressed in cream-coloured satin pyjamas. 'What are you doing up at this hour?' he said, surprised his voice came out so even when his heart was still thumping like a mad thing.

Even though it was dark, except for the moonlight, he could see the twin streaks of colour over her pale cheeks. 'I couldn't sleep...' she said. 'I came down for a glass of water and I thought I heard something.'

'You weren't frightened?'

She captured her lower lip between her teeth. 'Only a little.'

Leandro could feel his body calculating the distance between their bodies—every organ, every cell registering her presence like radar picking up a signal. He didn't trust himself to be near her. Not since he'd kissed her. *God, he had to stop thinking about that kiss.*

He could see every line of her slim body beneath the close-fitting drape of the satin pyjamas she was wearing. He could smell the freesia scent of her perfume. He could still taste her in his mouth—that alluring sweetness and hint of innocence that made him hard as stone. Her auburn hair was all mussed up, as if she had been tossing and turning in bed. He wanted to slide those silky strands through his fingers and to breathe in their clean, fresh fragrance. Her skin was luminous in the moonlight, her toffee-brown eyes shining like wet paint. He surged with blood when she moistened her mouth with the quick dart of her tongue. Was she remembering their kiss? Reliving it the way he had been doing for the last couple of hours? Feeling the desire licking along her veins as it had along his until he was almost crazy with it?

'Do you want a glass of milk or something?' he said, leading the way out of the room.

She screwed up her mouth like a child refusing to take medicine. 'I'm not much of a milk drinker.'

'Something stronger, then?'

'No, I'll just head back to bed,' she said. 'I'm sorry for disturbing you.'

'You weren't disturbing me.' He let out a short sigh as he closed the door behind him. 'I was just...remembering.'

Her eyes glistened as if she was about to cry. 'It must be so terribly hard for you, being here again.'

Leandro knew he shouldn't touch her. Touching her was dangerous. Touching her made it harder to keep his resolve in place. But even so his hand reached out and gently tucked a flyaway hair back behind the shell of her ear. He heard her draw in a sharp little breath, her mouth parting slightly, her eyes flicking downwards to his mouth. 'Don't tear yourself up about that kiss,' he said.

Her eyes skittered away from his. 'I'm not. I've forgotten all about it.'

He inched up her chin, holding her gaze with his. 'I can't *stop* thinking about it.'

She rolled her lips together. Blinked. Swallowed. Blinked again. 'You shouldn't do that.'

'Why not?'

'Because it's not right.'

He slid his hand along her cheek, cradling her face as his thumb moved over the silky skin of her face. 'It felt pretty right to me.' Which was the problem in a big, fat, inconvenient nutshell. It felt so damn right he wanted to do it again.

And not just kiss her. He wanted her like he had never wanted anyone. He felt it in his body now—the thunder of his blood heading south. The tingle in his thighs made him want to bring her close enough for her body to feel him. To feel the need he had for her. The hunger that would not go away now it had been awakened. Would she pull away or would she lean in like she had when he'd kissed her earlier? Would her body press urgently against his? Would she make those breathless little gasps of approval as his mouth showed her what it was like to kiss a full-blooded man?

She swept her tongue over her lips in a nervous manner. 'Just because something feels right doesn't make it right.'

Leandro moved his hand on her face to brush the pad of his thumb across her lower lip. 'Are you seriously going to spend the rest of your life being celibate?' he said.

A glitter of hauteur shone in her gaze as it held his. 'I find that imminently preferable to hooking up with people for no other reason than to slake animal lust.'

Was it just sisterly, friendly concern or was she jealous? 'Ah, so Nicole is an issue for you, then?'

Her mouth tightened to a flat disapproving line. 'It's no business of mine if you call her and sleep with her. You can call and sleep with anyone you like.'

'But you would hate it if I did.'

She stepped back from him and folded her arms across the front of her body, reminding him of a starchy schoolmistress from his childhood. 'Don't you want more out of life than that?' she said.

'Don't you?'

She pursed her lips. 'We're not talking about me.'

'No,' he said. 'Because talking about you makes you feel uncomfortable, doesn't it? You're happier dishing out the advice to everyone else while you turn a blind eye to your own needs.'

'You know nothing about my needs,' she flashed back.

He raised one of his brows. 'Are you sure about

that, Sleeping Beauty?' he said. 'I can still taste those needs in my mouth.'

Her cheeks flamed with colour. 'Why are you doing this?'

He took her by the shoulders gently but firmly. 'You're living a lie, Miranda. You know you are. A big, fat lie. You want more but you're too afraid to grow up and ask for it.'

She pulled away from him with a twist of her body, glaring at him. 'Did Julius put you up to this?'

Leandro frowned. 'Why do you say that?'

'He gave me one of his lectures recently,' she said. 'He said the same thing you said—that Mark would've moved on if the tables were turned. It's kind of telling, how you're suddenly taking an interest in me after ignoring me for all these years.'

'I haven't been ignoring you.' *Far from it*, he thought wryly. His awareness of her had been gradual, admittedly. He had always seen her as his mates' little sister. But over time he had watched her blossom from an awkward teenager into a beautiful and accomplished young woman. He noticed the way her creamy cheeks blushed when she was embarrassed, especially for some reason when he was around. He noticed her body; how it made his feel when she was in the same room as him. He noticed her slightest movement: the shy lick of her lips; the downward cast of her gaze; the nervous swallow; the sinking of her small white teeth into the blood-red pillow of her lower lip.

Leandro came to where she was standing with

her arms folded. 'I'm not ignoring you now,' he said, watching as the dark ink of her pupils flared.

She closed her eyes in a slow blink. 'Don't...'

'Don't what?'

The tip of her tongue sneaked out to moisten her lips. 'You're making this so hard for me...'

'Because you want to know what it feels like to be with a man instead of a boy, don't you?' Leandro said. 'That's why you kissed me the way you did. You didn't kiss like some shy little teenager who didn't know what she was doing. You kissed like a hot-blooded, passionate woman because that's who you really are underneath that prim and proper, twin-set-and-pearls façade you insist on hiding behind.'

Her mouth flattened to a thin line of white. 'You know something?' she said. 'I think I preferred it when you ignored me. I'm going to bed. Good night.'

Leandro muttered a stiff curse as she stalked off down the shadowed corridor until she disappeared from sight.

Miranda got to work on the collection first thing. She sorted the paintings into different sections for proper packing and shipping. She had already consulted her associates on one or two paintings that were outside her range of experience. By lunchtime she had done half the collection but that still left the other half, as well as the antiques.

She hadn't seen or heard from Leandro since late last night. She had gone to bed in a fit of temper over him pushing her to admit her needs. Needs she was perfectly happy ignoring, thank you very much. Or she had been, until he'd come along and stopped *ignoring* her. Grr! Was that why he had kissed her in the lane? Just to prove a point? To show her how it felt to kiss a man?

Well, she knew now. It felt good. It felt amazing. It felt so damn amazing she didn't know how she had managed to keep out of his arms last night. She had come close to throwing herself at him. Terrifyingly, shamelessly close. She had looked at his mouth and imagined it pressed on hers, his tongue doing all those wicked things it had done before, and the way hers had responded so wantonly.

Miranda didn't even know if he was still in the villa or whether he had left to meet Nicole. The thought of him with the other woman was like a stone in the pit of her belly.

Would he tell Nicole of the pain he held inside him? Would he share the agony of his childhood? The terrible loss he had experienced? The guilt and torment he still felt? Would he tell her about the estrangement he had suffered from his father and the distant relationship he had with his mother?

Or would they just have monkey sex without any emotional connection at all?

Miranda decided to get out of the villa for a while before she went mad over-thinking about Leandro's sex life. She bought some things for dinner and stopped for a coffee in a café that overlooked the stunning blue of the ocean. It was another mild day with soap-sud clouds gathering on the horizon. Although the late

summer crowds had well and truly gone, she was surprised to see only a couple of people swimming in the
sea, for the water temperature at this time of year was
warmer than in many parts of England in high summer.

Miranda wondered exactly where along the shore
Rosie had gone missing. The villa was only a few
blocks back from the seafront. She didn't know whether
she should ask Leandro to show her. Would it be too
painful for him to revisit that tragic spot?

As she walked back to the villa Miranda passed a
mother with a baby strapped in a pouch against her
chest with a little boy of about two in a pushchair. The
baby was sound asleep with its little downy head cradled against its mother's chest. The little toddler was
holding a brightly coloured toy and smiled at Miranda
as she navigated her way past on the narrow footpath.

Miranda resisted the urge to turn and look back at
the little family. When she'd been in her teens, seeing mums with kids hadn't been an issue. Even in the
weeks and months after Mark had died she had put the
thought out of her mind.

But now every time she saw a mother with a baby
she felt a pang, like a nagging toothache.

She would never have a baby of her own.

Somehow that had seemed like a romantic sacrifice when she'd been sixteen, sitting at Mark's bedside
with his life draining away in front of her eyes. Now at
twenty-three she felt as if the promise was a prison sentence—one without any possibility of parole. How was
she going to feel at thirty-three? Forty-three? Fifty?

Miranda pushed the thought to the back wall of her

mind. There were other things she had to concentrate on just now. Like how to get Leandro's father's collection safely shipped to London and the villa packed up ready for sale.

The villa was quiet when Miranda came in. She put her shopping away and then went up the stairs, but instead of going to her room as she had intended she found herself turning to Rosie's instead.

She opened the door and stood there for a moment. The toys were as they had been last night. The bed was still neatly made, all Rosie's things still on the dressing table.

Leandro had intimated he wanted the room to be packed up. Should Miranda do it to save him the pain? *Could* she do it?

Miranda wandered over to the cherry-wood wardrobe and, opening it, looked at the array of neat little hangers with toddler clothes. She ran her fingers along the different fabrics, wondering how any parent could ever navigate the loss of a child. Was there any way of dealing with such overwhelming grief? No wonder Leandro's father had left Rosie's things as they were. Packing them away was so final. So permanent.

Miranda closed the wardrobe with a sigh.

Leandro could smell something delicious as soon as he came into the villa. It was such a homely smell it took him aback for a moment. It had been a long time since he had felt as if this place was anything like a home. But with the sound of dishes clattering in the kitchen and Miranda moving about he got a sense of what the villa could one day be again with the right family. He imagined children coming in from the garden, as he and Rosie had done, their faces shining with exertion and sunshine. He could picture the evening meal with the family gathered around the kitchen table or in the dining room, everyone relating how their day had gone, the parents looking fondly at their children.

His parents hadn't been one-hundred percent happy with each other but they had loved him and Rosie.

Life had seemed so normal and then suddenly it wasn't.

Leandro walked into the kitchen to see Miranda popping something in the oven. She was wearing a cute candy-striped apron around her waist and her hair was tied up in a knot on top of her head. Her cheeks were flushed from the oven but they went a shade darker when she saw him standing there.

She swiped a strand of hair back from her face. 'Dinner won't be long.'

'You didn't have to cook,' he said. 'We could've eaten out or got takeaway.'

'I like cooking.' She rinsed her hands under the tap and dried them on a tea towel. 'So how was your date with Nicole? I presume that's where you've been? Did it all go according to plan?'

'We had a drink.'

Miranda's neat brows lifted. 'Just a drink?'

He held her gaze for a long beat, watching as a host of emotions flitted across her face. 'Yes. Just a drink.'

'You must be losing your touch.'

'Maybe.'

She began to fuss over a salad she was making on the counter. 'I've packed up about half of your father's paintings. I've still got some research to do on the others. I'm waiting to hear back from one of my colleagues. I should have it more or less done by the end of next week, maybe even earlier. I've got the shipping people on standby but I'll need you to authorise the insurance.'

Leandro felt something in his chest slip at the thought of her leaving earlier than he had planned. Had he pushed her too far? Made her feel uncomfortable? All he had wanted to do was make her see how she was throwing her life away… Well, maybe that wasn't all he wanted to do. He couldn't get the memory of their kiss out of his head. He kept reliving it. Kept feeling the sensual energy of it in his body. Every time he looked at her mouth he felt a spark fire in his groin. Did she feel it too? Was that why she was talking so quickly and keeping her eyes well away from his? 'Do you want me to change your flight back home?'

She caught her lip with her teeth, her gaze still avoiding his as she fiddled with the salad she was preparing. 'Do you want me to leave early?'

'No, but what do you want?'

She reached for an avocado and pressed it to see if it was ripe. 'I thought I'd stay on. Help you with the clean-up and stuff.'

'You don't have to.'

'I know, but I'd like to.'

'Why?'

She still actively avoided his gaze. 'I'm enjoy-

ing being out of London and not just because of the
weather. I can actually walk down the street here without anyone bothering me.'

'Always a bonus, I guess.'

Her cheeks went a faint shade of pink as she reached
for some cherry tomatoes. 'Will you be seeing Nicole
again before she leaves?'

Leandro couldn't help teasing her. 'For a drink, you
mean?'

'For…whatever.'

'No.'

Her brow puckered as she looked at him. 'Why not?'

Leandro hadn't intended to resume his on-off relationship with Nicole in any case but he found it amus-
ing to see Miranda struggle with the notion of him
having a sex life. Was she just being a prude or was
she actually jealous? Was she envisaging having a fling
with him? Maybe she thought she could get away with
it while she was away from home. Was that why she
kept looking at him with that hungry look in her eyes?
Was she rethinking her commitment to her dead boyfriend? Was she finally accepting it was time to move
on and live life in the present instead of in the past?
Could her fuss over Leandro's love life be a sign she
was finally ready to take that first step?

The thought of exploring the spark between them
was tempting.

More than tempting.

How long could he ignore the chemistry that swirled
in the air when he was in the same room as her? But

having a fling with her? How would he explain it to her brothers? It was a line he had sworn he would never cross. Not that he had ever discussed it with Julius or Jake. He hadn't even thought of Miranda that way. He wasn't sure when things had changed—when *he* had changed—but he had started to notice her quiet beauty. The way she moved. The way she spoke. The care and concern she expressed to those she loved. He had held back, kept his distance, not wanting to compromise his relationship with her brothers, or indeed with her.

And yet now he had kissed her. Touched her. Wanted her. How could he simply ignore the attraction he felt for her? Did he want to keep on ignoring it?

Could he ignore it?

Leandro gave a nonchalant shrug. 'It's time to move on.'

Her frown of disapproval deepened. 'So she's past her use-by date?'

'It's how it works these days.'

'I know, but it sounds pretty clinical if you ask me,' Miranda said. 'What if she was secretly hoping for more?'

He reached across for a piece of carrot. 'I make a point of never offering it in the first place.'

'But what if you change your mind?'

He gave her a pointed look. 'Like you might, do you mean?'

Her eyes fell away from his as she put the last touches to the salad. 'I'm not going to change my mind.'

'You sure about that, *ma belle*?'

Her small, neat chin came up. 'Yes.'

Leandro gave her another slanted smile. 'You're a determined little thing, aren't you?'

Miranda handed him the salad bowl. 'You'd better believe it.'

CHAPTER SIX

MIRANDA HAD BEEN asleep for a couple of hours when she woke with a sudden start. Had she heard something? She lay there for a moment, wondering if she had been dreaming that plaintive cry. Her sleep had been somewhat restless. Her visit to Rosie's room earlier that day, as well as seeing the mother with her baby and toddler, had made Miranda's slumbering mind busy with nonsensical narratives. Had she imagined that pitiless cry? Was the villa haunted by Rosie's ghost?

Miranda threw off the covers and padded to the door, listening with one ear for any further sound. Her heart was beating like a tattoo, the hairs on the back of her neck lifting as the old house creaked and groaned and resettled into the silence of the night.

It was impossible to go back to sleep. Even though in broad daylight she would swear she didn't believe in anything paranormal, it was a tough call in the middle of the night with shadows and sounds she couldn't account for. She pulled on a wrap, tied it about her waist and went out to the corridor. A shaft of pallid moonlight divided the passage. A branch of a tree scratched at the window nearest her, making her skeleton tingle inside the cage of her skin.

She tiptoed along the corridor but stopped when she got outside Leandro's room. There was a thin band of light shining underneath the door, not bright enough to be the centre light, but more like that of a lamp. There was no sound from inside the room. No sound of a computer keyboard being tapped or the pages of a book being turned.

Just a thick cloak of silence.

'Did you want something?' Leandro said from behind her.

Miranda swung around with her heart hammering so loud she could hear it like a roaring in her ears. 'Oh! I—I thought you were…someone else… I heard something. A cry. Did you hear it?'

'It's a cat.'

'A c-cat?'

'Yes, outside in the garden,' he said. 'There are a few strays around. I think my father must've been feeding them.'

Miranda rubbed her upper arms with her crossed-over hands. *A cat*. Of course it was a cat. How had she got herself so worked up? She didn't even believe in ghosts and yet…and yet she had been so sure that cry had been a small child crying out. 'Oh, right; well, then…'

Leandro looked at her keenly. 'Are you okay?'

She forced a brief tight smile. 'Of course.'

'Sure?'

Miranda licked her dry lips. 'I'd better get back to bed. Goodnight.'

He stalled her by placing a warm hand on her arm. She looked up into his shadowed face and felt her heart do another jerky somersault. She could smell the clean male scent of him, the wood and citrus blend and his own body heat that made her senses spin in dazed circles. His hair was ruffled, as if he had recently ploughed his fingers through it. It made her fingers ache to do the same, to feel those thick, silky strands against her fingertips.

His gaze was trained on her mouth. She felt the searing burn of it as if he had leaned down and pressed his sculptured lips to hers. Every nerve in her body was standing at attention, primed in anticipatory excitement.

'I thought you might be coming to tell me you've changed your mind,' he said.

She gave an involuntary swallow. 'A-about what?'

His eyes gleamed in the darkness, the moon catching the light of desire that blazed there as surely as it did in hers. 'About what you've been thinking from the moment I ran into you at that café in London.'

Miranda pulled a shutter down in her brain as she forced herself to hold his gaze. How could he possibly know what images her wayward mind kept conjuring up? How could he possibly sense the turmoil going on in her body? How could he know of the rampaging fire scorching through her veins at being this close to him? Or of the deep pulsating ache that was spreading through her thighs and pressing down between her legs? 'I'm not thinking...*that*.'

His mouth took on a sardonic slant. 'You're a terrible liar.'

Miranda forgot to breathe as he upped her chin, stroking his thumb against the swell of her lower lip until her senses were reeling. The temptation of his tantalising touch, his alluring proximity and the needs she was desperately trying to control were like a tug of war inside her body. Every organ shifted and strained against the magnetic pull of his flesh but it was too much. It was too powerful to resist. She felt her resolve collapsing like a humpy in a hurricane.

She didn't know who had closed that tiny space between their bodies but suddenly she was in his arms and his mouth was on hers in a passionate collision. The scrape of his stubble against her face made something slip sideways in her stomach. His deep, husky groan of pleasure as their tongues met and mated made her skin lift in delight.

Miranda couldn't control her response to his kiss. It suddenly didn't matter that she was supposed to be keeping her distance. Nothing mattered except tasting the warm, minty perfection of his mouth. Nothing mattered but feeling alive in his arms, feeling wanted, needed and desired. It was like a floodgate had opened up inside her. Her arms wound around his neck, her body pressed up close to the hot, hard heat of his as his lips moved with mind-blowing power on hers. She could feel the swell of his erection against her body, the exciting prospect of his potency triggering the release of intimate moisture within the secret cave of womanhood.

His tongue tangled with hers, teasing and cajoling it into seductive play with his. His arms were wrapped around her tightly, holding her as if he never wanted to let her go. Her flesh sang with the feel of him so aroused against her. It shocked her to realise how much she wanted him, how quickly it happened and how consuming it was to have the pulse of desire racing through her, skittling every sensible or rational objection out of the way.

Her mind was not in control now. Her body was on autopilot—hungry for the satiation of need. She hadn't thought herself capable of such intense passion. Of such wanton abandon that she would be breathlessly locked in Leandro's arms in a darkened corridor with her throat releasing little gasps and groans of encouragement as his mouth worked its breath-snatching magic on hers. How could one kiss do this to her? How could he have such sensual power over her?

His hands glided down her body, settling on her hips to keep her close to the throb of his arousal. All she could think was of how different he felt.

How *adult* he felt.

She could feel the swollen ridge of him against her belly, a spine-melting reminder of all that was different between them and how much she wanted to experience those differences. The intention of his body was clear—he wanted her. Her body was sending the same message back.

Miranda sent her fingers through the thickness of

his hair while her mouth stayed fused to his. One of his hands moved from her hip to settle in the small of her back, bringing her even closer to the thickened heat and throbbing pulse of his body. His blood pounded against her belly, ramping up her need until she was trembling with it. Had she ever felt such a thrill of the flesh? She had never been so aware of her body and how it reacted to the promise of fulfilment. It was like discovering a part of herself she hadn't known existed. A secret, passionate part that wanted, craved, needed. Hungered.

His mouth moved from hers to blaze a trail of fire down the sensitive skin of her neck, the sexy rasp of his stubble making her insides turn over. His tongue found the scaffold of her collarbone, dipping in and out of the shallow dish it created on her flesh. The grazing sensation of his tongue against her smooth skin made her knees loosen until she wondered if she would melt into a pool at his feet. Never had she felt such tremors course through her body. Such shudders and quakes of need that made everything inside her shake loose from its foundations.

'I want you,' Leandro said, his lips moving against her skin like a teasing brushstroke. 'But you've probably guessed that by now.'

Miranda shivered as his mouth came back up to just behind her ear. Every nerve danced as the tip of his tongue created sensual havoc. Where was her willpower? Where was her resolve? It was swamped, enveloped by a need that was clawing at her as his lips skated over her tingling flesh. How could she say no when every cell in her body was pleading for his possession?

Was this why she had hidden behind her commitment to Mark, because of the way Leandro made her feel? The way he had *always* made her feel? She had always been aware of him. Of his quiet strength. Of his heart-stopping attractiveness. Of his arrant maleness that made her female flesh shiver every time he came close.

How was she supposed to resist this assault on her senses? How was she to resist this urgent, primal call of her flesh?

'We shouldn't be doing this…' Her voice came out as a whispery thread that was barely audible. *I shouldn't be doing this.*

Leandro nudged her mouth with his lips, not touching down this time but close enough for their breaths to mingle. 'But you want to,' he said. 'I can feel it in your body. You're trembling with it.'

Miranda tried to still the tumult in her flesh but it was like trying to keep a paper boat steady in a hot tub. How could she deny it? How could she ignore the urgings of her flesh? Her whole body vibrated with clawing need. It moved through her body like a roaring tide. She could feel the pulse of lust low in her core—the hollow ache of need refused to be ignored. Her gaze went to his mouth, her belly doing a flip-turn as she thought of those warm, firm lips on her breasts, on her inner thighs. 'I made a promise…'

He pulled back to look at her. 'When you were a *kid*,

Miranda,' he said. 'You're a woman now. You can't ignore those needs. They're normal and healthy.'

Miranda had ignored those needs for so long but it
hadn't really been all that hard to do so. She had never
felt she was sacrificing anything. But now Leandro had
stirred those needs into life, awakened them from a
deep slumber. Sent them into a dizzying frenzy. How
could she pretend they weren't clamouring inside her
body? How could she deny the primal urges of her
body when his presence evoked such a storm within
her flesh? A storm she could feel rumbling through
her from where his hands were holding her. Burning
through her skin. Searing her so she would never be
able to forget his touch. Her body would always remember. Her lips would always recall the weight and
pressure of his. If she were never kissed by anyone
again it would be Leandro's kiss she would remember, not Mark's. It would be Leandro's touch her body
would recall and ache and hunger to feel again.

Would it be so wrong to indulge her senses just
this once? He wasn't offering her a relationship. He
had made it clear he didn't want the happy-ever-after.
But then, she couldn't—*wouldn't*—give it to him if
he wanted it.

But for this brief moment in time they could connect
in a way they had never connected before.

Miranda closed the small distance between their
bodies, a shockwave of awareness jolting through her
at the erotic contact. She watched as desire flared in his
gaze, burning with an incendiary heat that was as powerful as the backdraught of a fire. She slid her hands

up the flat plane of his chest, feeling the deep thud of his heart under her palm. She knew he wouldn't take this a step further until she had verbalised her consent. But she didn't want to say the words. She didn't want to own the earthy needs of her body. That would be admitting she was at the mercy of her flesh. That she was weak, frail, human.

Leandro held her gaze with the force field of his. 'Tell me you want me.'

Miranda drew his head back down, her mouth hovering within a breath of his. 'Kiss me.'

'Say it, Miranda,' he commanded.

She stepped up on tiptoe so her lips touched his, trying to distract him, to disarm him. 'Why are we talking when we could be doing other stuff?'

He gripped her by the upper arms in a firm but gentle hold. 'I'm not doing the other stuff until I know it's what you want. That we're clear on where this is going.'

Miranda looked into his implacable gaze. Desire burned in his eyes; she could feel it scorching her through her skin where his hands were cupped around her flesh. 'It doesn't have to go anywhere,' she said. 'It can just be for now.'

His ever-present frown deepened a fraction. 'And you'd be okay with that?'

She would have to be okay. How could she say she wanted more when for all these years she had told everyone she didn't? She had taught herself not to want more. She had blocked all thoughts of a fairy-tale romance, of being married, of one day having a baby, of raising a family with the man she loved, because the man she had loved had died.

But this was a chance to live a little. To break free of the restraints she had set around herself. It didn't have to go anywhere. It didn't have to last. It *couldn't* last.

It was for the moment.

Miranda traced her fingertip over the dark stubble surrounding his mouth, her insides quivering as she felt the graze of his flesh against the pad of her finger. 'Neither of us wants anything permanent,' she said. 'This would be just something that…happened.'

'So you only want it to happen here?' he said. 'While we're in France?'

A French fling. A secret affair. A chance to play while no one was looking. No one need know. Her brothers, her parents, Mark's parents—even Jaz—didn't need to know. It would be over before it began. There wouldn't be time for things to get complicated. No one was making any promises. No one was falling in love. This would change the dynamic of their relationship, certainly, but as long as they were both clear on the boundaries then why not indulge their attraction for each other?

'That would be best, don't you think?' she said.

Leandro searched her gaze for a long moment. 'You don't want your brothers to know about us?'

Miranda bit down on her lip. 'Not just them…'

'Mark's family?'

She let out a breath. 'Look, if you're having second thoughts—'

'I'm not, but I'm wondering if you are,' he said. 'If not now, then later.'

Miranda saw the concern in his dark-as-night gaze. What was he worried about? That she would get all clingy and suddenly want more than he was prepared to give? She knew the rules. He had made them perfectly clear. She was okay with it. Totally okay. More than okay. 'I'm a big girl, Leandro. I can take responsibility for my decisions and actions.'

He brushed a strand of hair back off her face, his expression cast in serious lines. 'I want you to know I didn't ask you here to have an affair with me. The thought didn't cross my mind.'

Miranda raised one of her brows. 'Not even once?'

His mouth took on a rueful angle. 'Well, maybe once or twice.' His arms came around her to draw her close. 'I've always kept my distance because I didn't want to compromise my relationship with your family. It gets messy when things don't work out. Look at Jake and Jasmine.'

Miranda traced his mouth with her fingertip again. 'Did Jake ever tell you what happened that night?'

'No,' he said, kissing the tip of her finger. 'What's Jasmine's version of events?'

'She refuses to discuss it,' Miranda said, suppressing a shiver as Leandro's tongue curled around her finger as he drew it into his mouth. The sucking motion of his mouth made her inner core pull tight with lust.

'Someone needs to lock them in a room together until they thrash it out,' he said as he began to scorch a pathway of kisses up her neck. She shuddered as his tongue outlined the cartilage of her ear, longing coursing through her body in sweeping waves. 'Speaking of being locked in a room together...'

He gathered her up in his arms and carried her inside his room. The lamp was already on, giving the room a muted glow. He set her on her feet but not before sliding her down the length of his body, leaving her in no doubt of his need. The feel of his erection against her made her desire for him escalate to a level she had never experienced before. A restless ache pulsed deep in her body, a hollow sensation that yearned to be filled. Her breasts became sensitive where they were pressed against the hard plane of his chest. She could feel the tight buds of her nipples abraded by the lace cups of her bra. She wanted to feel his hands on her naked flesh, his mouth, his lips and his masterful tongue.

Miranda sucked in a breath as he slid his hands up under her top, the warmth of his palms against her skin sending her senses reeling. His hand came to the sensitive underside of her breast, stilling there as if to give her time to prepare for a more intimate touch. She moved against him, silently urging him to touch her.

'You're so beautiful,' he said.

Miranda had always felt a little on the small side, especially since her mother was so well-endowed. But Leandro's touch made her feel as if she was the most gorgeously proportioned woman he had ever touched.

He brought his mouth down to her right breast in a gentle caress that made her spine tingle from top to bottom. He circled her tight nipple with his tongue before he swept it over the underside of her breast where every nerve fizzed and leapt in response.

He came back to take her nipple in his mouth, drawing on her with just the right amount of suction. A frisson of excitement shot down between her legs, pooling in the warm, moist heart of her body. She had never felt desire like it. Her body had developed cravings and capabilities she'd had no idea it possessed. Never had she felt such intense ripples of delight go through her flesh.

He switched his attention to her other breast, leaving no part of it unexplored by his lips and tongue. The electric sensations ricocheted through her body, making her utter little gasping cries as he came back to cover her mouth.

His kiss was purposeful, passionate, consuming. His tongue came in search of hers, stroking, caressing and conquering, delighting her senses, stirring her passion to an even higher level.

Miranda threaded her fingers through his hair, stroking the back of his neck, going lower to his shoulders and back. She brought her hands around to the front of his shirt, undoing his buttons with more haste than efficiency. He shrugged himself out of it before helping her with her pyjama top. She watched as his eyes feasted on her naked form but, instead of feeling shy and inadequate, she felt feminine and beautiful.

He brought his mouth down to each of her breasts, subjecting them to another passionate exploration that made her insides shudder with longing. She made breathless little sounds of approval, her lower body on fire as it sought the intimate invasion of his.

Her hands glided down his chest, exploring the sculpted perfection of his toned body. She came to the waistband of his jeans, shyly skating her hand over the potent bulge below. He reached down and unfastened his jeans so her hand could go lower. Miranda took up the invitation with new-found boldness, delighting in the feel of his tautly stretched skin, thrilled by the way his body responded to her with every glide and stroke of her fingers. Moisture oozed from him as her thumb moved over the head of his penis, that most primal signal of the readiness to mate. She could feel her own moisture gathering between her legs, the deep, low ache of need throbbing with relentless urgency.

He gently eased her out of her pyjama bottoms, sliding them down her thighs with reverent care. She snatched in a hitching breath when his fingertip traced the seam of her body. His touch was so light, so careful, yet it stirred every nerve in her body into a riotous happy dance.

'I don't want to rush you,' he said.

Rush me! Rush me! Miranda silently pleaded. 'You're not… It's just…been a while.'

Leandro meshed his gaze with hers. 'I want to make it good for you. Tell me what you like.'

Anything you do will be just fine, Miranda thought. Even the way he looked at her was enough to send her senses into the stratosphere. 'I'm not very good at this…'

His brows came together. 'You *have* had sex, haven't you?'

She moved her gaze out of reach of his. 'Yes, of course…'

He gently inched up her chin so her eyes came back to his. 'But?'

Miranda moistened her lips, suddenly feeling shy and hopelessly inadequate again. What a pariah he would think her. So inexperienced she didn't know what worked for her and what didn't. How could she tell him she hadn't had an orgasm other than on her own? That she had found sex a bit one-sided? He would think her a prude, an unsophisticated Victorian throwback. She bet the women he dated—the Nicoles—would know exactly what worked for them and what didn't. They would be totally comfortable with their bodies and its needs. They would know what to say and what to do. They wouldn't be feeling gauche and stupid and useless because they had never had satisfying sex with a partner.

'Miranda?' Leandro prompted softly, his dark eyes holding hers.

Miranda drew her lower lip into her mouth, pressing down on it with her top one. 'It wasn't always good for me with Mark,' she said at last. 'It wasn't his fault. We were both inexperienced. I should've said something earlier. But then he got sick and I just let him do what he needed.'

Leandro's frown was a solid bar across his eyes. 'Did you ever come with him?'

She could feel her cheeks heating up like a radiator. 'No…'

He cupped the side of her face in one of his broad but gentle hands, his thumb moving back and forth in a slow, measured way. 'So you're practically a virgin,' he said.

Miranda lowered her gaze. 'I know you probably think that's ridiculous…that *I'm* ridiculous.'

He continued to stroke her hot cheek, his gaze soft as it held hers. 'I don't think that at all,' he said. 'It's not always easy for young women to get their needs met. Men can be insensitive and ignorant and selfish. That's why communication is so important.'

Miranda looked into the warmth of his coal-black gaze and wondered how she was going to keep her heart secure. He was so considerate, so understanding and so deeply insightful. Hadn't she always sensed he was a cut above other men? Why was he wasting himself on shallow relationships when he had so much to offer? He was 'life partner' material. The sort of man who would stand by his partner through thick and thin. He would be dependable, loyal and trustworthy. He would put his partner's needs before his own. Like he was doing now. He was taking the time to understand her. Treating her with the utmost respect and consideration.

She put her hand against his jaw, her skin tingling at the contact of his stubble. 'Make love to me,' she said in a soft whisper.

He leaned down to kiss her in a lingering exchange that made her body tremble in anticipation. His hands moved over her with tenderness but with the undercurrent of passion. Excitement coursed through her from head to toe, her breathing becoming faster, more urgent, as he stoked the fire of her desire. Sensations flooded her being, showers of them, cascades of them, great, spilling fountains of them that made her feel she had been sleepwalking through life until now.

He kissed his way from her mouth to her belly button, dipping his tongue into its tiny cave before going lower. She forgot to breathe when he came to her folds. His tongue moved down the seam of her body, tracing her without separating her. Fireworks erupted under her skin at the feel of his warm breath skating over her.

He gently separated her with his fingers, waiting for her to take a steadying breath before he put his mouth to her. A host of insecurities rushed through her brain. *Was she fresh enough? Was she waxed enough? Did she look normal? Was he comparing her to his other lovers?*

Leandro placed his hand on her belly in a stabilising manner. 'Relax for me, *cara*,' he said. 'Stop fretting. You're beautiful. Perfect.'

How could he read her mind as well as her body? Miranda wondered. But then she stopped thinking altogether as he put his mouth to her again. His tongue tasted and tantalised her, stroking and caressing her into spine-loosening delight. The tension inside her body built to a breaking point. It was like climbing a mountain only to be suspended at the edge of the precipice. Hovering there. Wavering. Teetering at that one tight, breath-robbing point, every cell in her body straining, pulling and contracting until finally she was pitched into the unknown. She felt like she was exploding into a thousand tiny fragments, like a party balloon full of glitter. Waves of pleasure washed over her, through her, tossing and tumbling her until she was spinning in a whirlpool of physical rapture.

Leandro came back over her to press a tender kiss to the side of her mouth. 'Good?'

Miranda could smell her own female scent on him. Such raw intimacy shocked her and yet somehow it felt right. She looked at him in a combination of wonder and residual shyness. 'You know it was.'

He kissed her on the lips, on the chin, on each of her eyelids and then back on her mouth. 'It'll get better when you feel more comfortable with me,' he said.

You'd better not get too comfortable, a little voice piped up inside her head.

Miranda ignored it as she moved underneath the delicious weight of his body, her senses stirring all over again at the thought of him possessing her fully. She reached down to caress him, stroking his turgid length with increasing confidence, watching as he showed his pleasure at her touch on his features and in the way he gave deep, growly groans in his throat.

He pulled back from her with a sucked-in breath. 'I'd better put on a condom.'

Miranda waited while he got one out of his wallet where it was sitting on the bedside chest-of-drawers. He sheathed himself before coming back over her, making sure she was comfortable with his weight by angling his body over hers. She stroked her hands down his back from the tops of his shoulders to the base of his spine, drawing him closer to the deep ache in her core.

He couldn't have been gentler as he entered her but

even so her breath caught at the sensation of him filling her. 'Am I hurting you?' he said, holding still.

She released a long, slow breath to help herself relax. 'No…'

'Sure?'

She smiled and stroked his lean, tanned jaw as she looked into his concerned gaze. 'You worry too much.'

He brushed her hair back from her forehead in a tender action. 'You're so tiny I feel like I'm going to break you.'

Something hot and liquid spilled and flowed in Miranda's belly. Could there be a man more in tune with a woman's sense of vulnerability? 'I'm tougher than I look,' she said, reaching up to kiss him on the lips.

He deepened the kiss as he moved within her, going in stages so she could have time to adjust to his length and width. He began to move in slow, rhythmic strokes, the gentle friction tantalising her senses, driving up her need until she was making soft little noises of encouragement in case he took it upon himself to stop. Miranda felt she would *die* if he stopped. The craving of her body rose to fever pitch. She felt it clawing at her, frantically trying to attain assuagement. She was almost there…poised to go over the edge but frustratingly unable to let go.

Leandro reached between their bodies, used his fingers to coax her and suddenly she was there, falling, falling, falling. Coming apart in a bigger and more intense way than before. Her body contracted around his, each spasm of her orgasm taking her to new even more exciting heights of pleasure.

She felt the exact moment he let go. He gave a low, deep groan and surged, his breath coming out in a hot gust against the side of her neck as he shuddered and emptied.

Miranda held him close, her hands moving over his muscled back and shoulders, massaging him, stroking and caressing him in that rare moment of male vulnerability.

She didn't know what to say so said nothing. Her senses were so dazed by the power of their physical connection it was impossible to articulate how she felt. She wondered why she didn't feel ashamed. She had broken her promise to Mark but how could she regret something so…so *magical* as Leandro's love-making? He had shown her what her body was capable of feeling. He had opened up a world of pleasure she hadn't known existed. Not like that. Not so powerfully consuming it had made her disconnect from her mind. Her body had taken over. Her primitive nature had driven her. Controlled her. Surprised her. Shocked her.

Leandro shifted his weight to his elbows to look at her. 'Hey.'

'Hey.' Her voice came out husky, whisper-soft.

He stroked his fingertip in a circle over her chin, his look rueful. 'I've given you beard rash.'

Miranda's breath caught on something. 'Just as well we're not around anyone we know,' she said lightly. 'Jaz would spot it in a heartbeat. I'd never hear the end of it.'

A frown created two pleats over his dark, serious eyes. 'You think she'd disapprove?'

Miranda recalled her conversation with her friend at

Jaz's bridal boutique. 'No,' she said. 'She thinks you've been interested in me for a while.'

Something flickered over his face like a wind rippling across sand. He moved away from her to dispose of the condom. It was a long moment before he met her gaze. 'I don't want you to think this is more than it is.'

She did her best to ignore the little jab of disappointment his words evoked. 'I know what this is, Leandro.'

He moved his tongue around the inside of his cheek as if he was rehearsing something before he said it. 'It's not that I don't care about you. I do. You're an incredibly special person to me. As are all of your family. But this is as far as it goes.'

Miranda got off the bed, dragging the sheet with her to cover her nakedness. 'Do we really need to have this conversation?' she said. 'We both know the rules. No one's going to suddenly move the goal posts.'

His expression was as inscrutable as that of one of the marble statues downstairs. 'You deserve more,' he said. 'You're young. Beautiful. Talented. You'd make someone a wonderful wife and mother.'

'I don't want those things any more,' she said. 'That dream was taken away. I don't want it with anyone else.' Even as she said the words Miranda wondered why they didn't sound as convincing as they once had. She had made that heartfelt promise just moments before Mark had died. *There will be no one else for me. Ever. I will always be yours.*

Mark's parents had been there with her at his bedside in ICU. The heart-wrenching emotion of saying goodbye, of watching as someone she loved took their last breaths, had made Miranda all the more determined to stay true to her promise. But now, as an adult, she wondered more and more if she had truly loved Mark enough to sign away her life. Or had his illness given her a purpose—a mission to follow that gave her life meaning, direction and significance?

She didn't know who she was without that mission. That purpose. It was too frightening to live without it. It had defined her, shaped her and motivated her for the last seven years.

Leandro made a sound of derision that scraped at her raw nerves. 'You're a fool to throw your life away for a selfish teenager who should've known better than to play with your emotions like that. For God's sake, Miranda, he didn't even have the decency to satisfy you in bed and yet you persist with this nonsense he was the love of your life.'

Miranda didn't want to hear Leandro vocalise what she was too frightened to think, to confront—to deal with. She drew in a scalding breath as she turned for the door. 'I don't have to listen to this. I know what I felt—*feel*.'

'That's right,' Leandro said. 'Run away. That's what you do when things cut a little close to the bone.'

She swung back to glare at him. 'Isn't that what *you* do, Leandro? You haven't been back here since you were a child. Your father died without you saying a proper goodbye to him. Doesn't that tell you something?'

His jaw clamped so tightly two spots of white appeared either side of his mouth. 'I wasn't welcome here. My father made that perfectly clear.'

Miranda dropped her shoulders on a frustrated sigh. How could he be so blind about his father? Couldn't he see what was right in front of his eyes? He was surrounded by everything his father had treasured the most: rooms and rooms full of wonderful, priceless pieces, paintings worth millions of pounds. Not to mention Rosie's things—her clothes and toys, the life-like statue in the garden—all left to Leandro's care. 'And yet he left you *everything*,' she said. 'Everything he valued he left to you. He could have donated it all to charity as you're threatening to do but he didn't. He left it all to you because you meant something to him. You were his only son. I don't believe he would've left you a thing if he didn't love you. He *did* love you. He just didn't know how to show it. Maybe his grief over Rosie got in the way.'

Leandro's throat rose and fell. He turned away to plough his fingers through his hair, the silence so acute she heard the scrape of his fingers against his scalp.

It seemed a decade before he spoke. 'I'd like to be alone.'

Miranda's heart gave a painful spasm at the rawness of his tone. What had made her speak so out of turn? She knew nothing of the heartbreak he had been through. She didn't know his father. She had never met him. She had no idea of how Leandro's relationship with him had operated. She was an armchair survivor. Leandro had every right to be furious with her. What right did she have to criticise his decision to stay away from his childhood home? He had suffered cruelly for his part in his sister's disappearance. A part he wasn't even responsible for, given he had been so young. 'I'm sorry,' she said. 'I should never have said what I said. It was insensitive and…'

'Please.' His voice was curt. 'Just leave.'

Miranda went over to him, undaunted by his terse tone. She didn't want to be dismissed. Pushed away. Rejected. She didn't want their wonderful physical connection to be overshadowed by an argument that should never have happened. What they had shared was too important. Too special to be tainted by a misunderstanding. She placed a gentle hand on his arm, looking up at his tautly set features. 'Please don't push me away,' she said. 'Not now. Not after what we shared.'

He looked at her for a beat or two before he placed his hand over hers where it was resting on his arm. He gave her hand a light squeeze, the line of his mouth rueful. 'You're right,' he said on the back end of a sigh. 'I should've come back before now.'

Miranda put her arms around him and held him close. 'You're back now,' she said, resting her cheek against his chest. 'That's all that matters.'

Leandro held her against him. 'It was hard…seeing him like that,' he said. 'Every time he came to London I had to prepare myself for spending time with him. No matter what time we agreed on meeting, he'd always been a couple of drinks down before I got there. Over the last couple of years it got progressively worse. He would sometimes be so drunk he would start crying and talking incoherently. Other times he would be angry and abusive. All I could think was it was my fault. That *I* had done that to him.'

Miranda looked up at him with tears in her eyes. 'It wasn't your fault.'

His look was grim. 'He never wanted me to come back here after the divorce. He made it clear he couldn't handle having a child around.'

'Maybe he was worried he wouldn't be able to look after you properly,' Miranda said. 'Maybe he just didn't know how to be a parent without having your mum around. Lots of divorced dads are like that, especially back then, when dads weren't so hands-on as they are now.'

'I let things slide as the years went on,' he said. 'Even as an adult it was easier to stay away than to come back and relive the nightmare. But I should've come back before now. I should've allowed my father to die with some measure of peace.'

Miranda hugged him close again. 'I'm not sure there's much peace to be had when you've lost a child. But at least you're doing what he wanted you to do— taking care of everything he left behind.'

He brushed one of his hands down the back of her head, his gaze meshing with hers. 'Don't go back to your room,' he said. 'Stay here with me.'

Miranda wondered if he was allowing her the dignity of not being dismissed now they had made love or whether he truly wanted her to spend the night with him. She didn't know what his arrangement was with other women but she hoped this invitation to sleep the whole night with him was a unique offer. 'Are you sure?' she said.

He lowered his mouth to within reach of hers. 'You don't take up much space. I bet I won't even notice you there.'

'Then I'll have to make sure you do,' Miranda said softly as his mouth came down and sealed hers.

CHAPTER SEVEN

LEANDRO HADN'T PLANNED to spend the night with Miranda but, just like when he had run into her in London, it had come out of his mouth as if his brain had no say in it at all. *So much for the rules*, he thought as he watched her sleeping. He never spent the full night with anyone. It wasn't just because he was too restless a sleeper. He didn't want to get too connected, too comfortable with having someone beside him when he woke up. He didn't allow himself to think of long, lazy mornings in bed. Not just making love but talking, dreaming, planning. Hoping.

She looked so beautiful his heart squeezed. Had he done the wrong thing in engaging in an affair with her? He had been so adamantly determined to keep his distance as he had always done in the past. But being alone with her changed everything. That first touch… that first heart-stopping kiss…had made him realise how deep and powerful their connection was. Hadn't he always sensed that connection? Wasn't that why he had respectfully kept clear of her? He hadn't wanted to start something he couldn't finish.

But now it *had* started.

He didn't want to think about how it was going to finish, but finish it must, as all his relationships did.

Her inexperience hardly put them on an equal footing. But he wanted her to realise how crazy it was to put a pause button on her life. He hated seeing her waste her potential because of a silly little schoolgirl promise that had been well meant but totally misguided. She was young—only twenty-three years old. At thirty-three, Leandro felt ancient in comparison. She was far too young to be living like a nun. Her whole life was ahead of her. She had experienced tragedy, yes, but it didn't mean she couldn't find happiness again—if in fact she had actually been happy with Mark Redbank.

The more Leandro reflected on that teenage relationship, the more he suspected how imbalanced it had been. Miranda was a sucker for romance. She had always been the type of girl who cried at soppy movies, or even at commercials with puppies or kittens in them. She had a big heart and gave it away all too easily. He didn't believe she had been truly in love with Mark. At sixteen who knew what they wanted or even who they were? She had wanted to feel special to someone and Mark had offered her that chance. Mark's parents had welcomed her into the bosom of their family and it had made her feel normal.

Normal was important to someone like Miranda. She didn't enjoy the notoriety of her father and mother and the baggage that came with it. Mark's illness had cemented her commitment to him but Leandro truly believed their relationship would not have lasted if Mark had survived.

But was sleeping with her himself going to convince her she was wasting her life?

He had crossed a boundary he couldn't uncross. Their relationship would never be the same. They could never go back to being platonic friends. The intimacy they had shared would always be between them. Would other people see it? Did it matter if they did? Her brothers might have something to say about it but only because they were protective of her. They might even be quite glad he had encouraged her to live a little.

He hadn't coerced her into sleeping with him. They were both consenting adults. He had given her plenty of opportunity to pull back. But he was glad she hadn't. Making love with her was different somehow. It wasn't just her lack of experience, although he'd be lying if he said it hadn't delighted him. It had given their union a certain quality he hadn't experienced with any other partner. Their love-making had had an almost sacred element to it. Or maybe it was because he had opened up a part of himself he had never opened before. He had never shared the pain of his childhood with anyone before. He had never shared his loss. He had never shared his guilt. He had never felt more exposed as a man, yet Miranda's gentle compassion had reached deep inside him like a soothing balm on a raw and seeping wound.

Miranda stirred in her sleep and he watched as the dark fans of her lashes flickered against her cheek. She slowly opened her eyes and blinked at him owlishly. 'What time is it?'

He brushed her mussed-up hair off her face. 'Three-thirty or so.'

She stroked one of her hands down his bare chest, making every cell in his body stand to attention. 'Couldn't you sleep?' she asked with a little frown of concern.

That was another thing that set her apart from his previous partners, Leandro thought. She genuinely cared about him. Worried about him. Put her needs and interests aside to concentrate on his. He smoothed her frown away with the blunt end of his thumb. 'I got a couple of hours.'

She lowered her gaze from his and tugged at her lower lip with her teeth. 'Is my being in your bed disturbing you?'

Leandro cupped her face, bringing her gaze back up to his. 'Only in a good way.'

Her cheeks developed a pink tinge. 'I could go back to my room if you'd like...'

He ran an idle fingertip from behind her ear to her chin, watching as she gave a little shiver, as if his touch had sent a current through her flesh. It thrilled him to think his touch did the same things hers did to him. That their bodies were so finely tuned to each other that the mere brush of a fingertip could evoke such a response. 'That would be a shame,' he said.

She licked her lips with a quick dart of her tongue, her toffee-brown eyes luminous. 'Why?'

'Because I wouldn't be able to do this,' he said, lowering his mouth to hers.

Her arms went around his neck as she gave herself

up to his kiss, her soft little sigh making his blood pound all the harder. He deepened the kiss with a stroke of his tongue against her lips and she opened on another sigh and nestled closer, her lower body searching for his. He put his hand on her naked bottom, drawing her to his straining erection. The feel of her skin on his skin made him want to break all of his rules. The condom rule in particular. But he never had unprotected sex. That was one line he never crossed. He pulled back to get one from his wallet, mentally making a note to replenish his supply.

Miranda looked at him with her clear brown gaze. 'Do you ever make love without a condom?'

'Never.'

'What about for oral sex?'

The thought of her gorgeous mouth surrounding him made him rock-hard. But he would never pressure her to do it. 'Always,' he said.

She rolled her lips together for a moment. 'Do you want me to…?'

'Not unless you want to,' he said. 'It's not for everyone.'

'But I'd like to,' she said, reaching for him, her soft little hand sending shivers up and down his spine. 'You pleasured me that way. I want to learn how to do it properly.'

'Did you do it with—?'

'No,' she said quickly, her gaze moving out of reach of his. 'I only ever used my hand.'

Leandro inched up her chin again. 'You don't need to feel bad about that. You should only ever do what you're comfortable with. No one should force or pressure you into doing something that doesn't feel right.'

She stroked her hand down the length of his shaft. 'I want to do it to you.'

His heart rate soared. His blood quickened. His skin peppered with anticipatory goose bumps. 'You don't have to.'

'I want to,' she said, sliding down his body, her warm breath teasing him as she positioned herself.

He drew in a sharp breath as she sent her tongue down him from the tip to the base. Her warm breath puffed over him as she came back up to circle her tongue around the head, her lips closing over him and then drawing on him. Even with a condom the sensations were electrifying, the sight of her so stimulating he had to fight hard for control. He tried to ease away to give her the chance to take a break but she hummed against him and held on, her mouth taking him over the edge into mind-blowing bliss.

He disposed of the condom once he could move again. His body was so satiated he felt like someone had undone every knob of his spine. Waves of lassitude swept through him, making him realise how long it had been since he had truly relaxed.

His sexual relationships had been pleasurable in a clinical, rather perfunctory way. He always made sure his partners got what they needed but sometimes he felt as if he was just going through the motions: drink, dinner, sex. It had become as simple and impersonal as that. He didn't linger over deep and meaningful conversations. He didn't spend the whole night with anyone.

He didn't allow himself to get that close. Close enough to want more. Close enough to need more.

But looking at Miranda beside him made him realise how much he was missing. His life was full of work and activity and yet…and yet deep down he felt something was missing. He had thought financial security would be enough. He had thought career success would satisfy him. But somehow it just made the empty space inside him seem bigger.

There was a canyon of dissatisfaction inside him. It echoed with the loneliness he felt, especially during the long hours of the night. He knew what would bridge it but he dared not risk it. He couldn't be part of a long-term relationship because he couldn't allow himself to risk letting someone down the way he had let Rosie and his parents down. How could he ever envisage a life with someone? A life with children was out of the question. How could he ever trust himself to keep them safe? He would always live with the gut-churning fear he might not be able to protect them. He had been responsible for so much heartache.

He couldn't bear to inflict more on anyone else.

Miranda lifted her fingertip to his face, tracing the line of his frown. 'Did I disappoint you?'

Leandro captured her hand and pressed his mouth to it. 'Why would you think that?'

'You went so still and quiet and you were frowning… I thought I must've done something wrong…'

He stroked his fingertip down the length of creamy cheek. 'You blew me away, literally and figuratively.'

Her eyes brightened and a smile tilted up the corners of her mouth. 'I did?'

He pressed her back down on the bed, hooking one of her legs over his. 'And now it's my turn to do the same to you.'

Miranda woke to bright sunlight pouring through the windows of Leandro's bedroom. She turned her head to the pillow beside her but, apart from the indentation of where his head had been, the space was empty. She sat up and brushed her sleep- and sex-tousled hair out of her face. When she swung her legs over the bed she felt a faint twinge of discomfort. Her inner muscles had experienced quite a workout last night. Leandro's love-making had been passionate and breathtakingly exciting and her body was still humming with aftershocks of pleasure.

It occurred to her it might not be so easy to put her fling with Leandro to one side when she returned to England. Would she blush every time she saw him, knowing he had pleasured every single inch of her body? That he alone knew exactly what made her cry out with ecstasy? That he alone knew what she looked like totally naked?

Would *he* look at her differently? Would he treat her differently? Would others notice? How on earth would she keep it a secret from Jaz? Or would Jaz guess as soon as she saw her?

Miranda went back to her own room to shower and dress. When she came downstairs she found Leandro in the study working on his laptop. He was so deep in concentration he didn't notice her at first. But then he looked up and his heavy frown was replaced with a brief smile. 'Sleep okay?' he said.

'Yes, but clearly you didn't.'

He stood and rubbed the back of his neck with one of his hands. 'I had some accounts to go through. It's a big job I'm working on for Jake. I need to get it sorted as soon as possible.'

Miranda slipped her arms around his waist and nestled against his tall, lean frame. 'You work too hard.'

He rested his chin on the top of her head as he drew her closer. 'How are you feeling?'

'Fine.'

He eased back to search her gaze with the intensely dark probe of his. 'Not sore?'

Miranda felt her cheeks heat up. 'A little.'

He stroked her cheek with a gentle fingertip, his expression rueful. 'I'm sorry.'

She pressed closer to link her arms around his neck, her pelvis flush against the hardness of his. 'I'm not.' She stepped up on tiptoe to brush her lips against his. 'You were wonderful.'

He looked down at her with that persistent frown between his brows. 'You don't regret getting involved like this?'

'Do you?'

He let out a long breath. 'I'm worried it will change our relationship,' he said. 'In a negative way, I mean.'

'We've always been friends, Leandro,' Miranda said. 'That's not likely to change just because we took it to a new level for a week or two.'

He continued to look at her in a contemplative manner. 'Do you think you'll date someone else when you get back?'

Miranda frowned. 'Why would I do that?'

'Because now you've broken the drought, so to speak.'

She slipped out of his hold and folded her arms across her middle, throwing him a hardened glance. 'So, I suppose you'll call Nicole once we're done?'

His eyes took on a flinty edge. 'I'm not sure why that should be such a sticking point for you.'

Miranda let out a whooshing breath. 'How can you settle for someone who just uses you to scratch an itch? How can you use her? Don't you want more than that?'

'Don't you?'

'I *hate* how you do that,' she said. 'You always shift the focus onto me because you're not comfortable talking about what it is you really want. You think you don't deserve to be happy because of what happened to your sister. It's. Not. Your. Fault. You didn't do anything wrong. Sacrificing your life won't change the past.'

His top lip curled. 'Will you listen to yourself? How about we play a little game of "it's hypothetical"? If I were to ask you to commit to a long-term relationship with me, would you do it?'

Miranda stared at him for a dumbstruck moment. 'I don't— I'm not— You're not—'

He gave a bark of cynical laughter. 'The answer is no, isn't it? You're too invested in living the role of the martyr. I bet you won't even tell your best friend what you got up to with me.'

Jaz will probably guess as soon as she sees me, Miranda thought. 'But you would never ask me to commit to you… Would you?'

'No.'

A sharp pain jabbed her under the ribs. Did he have to be so blunt? So adamant? 'Wow,' she said with a hint of scorn. 'You really know how to boost a girl's self-esteem.'

He swung away to stand with his back to her as he looked out of the window. He drew in a deep breath and let it out in a halted stream. 'I knew this would be a mistake. I have this amazing ability to ruin every relationship I enter into.'

Miranda couldn't bear to see him so tortured with such guilt and self-blame. Her heart ached for him. He was so torn up with regret and self-recrimination. He was so alone in his suffering, yet she wanted to stand by him, to help him work his way through it to a place of peace. She stepped up to him and stroked her hand down the tightly clenched muscles of his back. He flinched as if her touch had sent an electric shock through him. 'You haven't ruined our relationship,' she said softly.

He put an arm around her and drew her close to the side of his body, leaning down to press a soft-as-air kiss to the top of her head. 'I'm sorry, *ma petite*,' he said. 'None of this is your fault. It's me. It's this wretched, bloody house. It's all the stuff I can't fix.'

Miranda looked up at him with compassion. 'Have you told Julius and Jake about your sister yet?'

'I emailed them a couple of days ago.'

'Did that help? Explaining it to them?'

'A bit, I guess,' he said. 'They were good about it. Supportive.'

A little silence passed.

'What about us?' she said. 'Did you tell them we were…?'

'No,' he said. 'Have you?'

Miranda shook her head. 'It's not that I'm ashamed or anything… I just don't feel comfortable discussing my sex life with my older brothers.'

'Fair enough.'

She waited another beat or two before asking, 'Will you take me to the place where Rosie went missing?'

His frown carved a deep trench in his forehead. 'Why?'

'Because it might help you get some closure.'

He turned his gaze back to the view outside the window but his arm was still around her. She felt it tighten momentarily, as if he had come to a decision inside his head. 'Yes…'

Leandro could feel his heart banging against his chest wall like a church bell struck by a madman. A cold sweat was icing down between his shoulder blades and his stomach was pitching as he walked to the place where Rosie and he had been sitting. The beach wasn't crowded like that fateful day in summer but the memories came flooding back. He could hear the sound of children playing—the sound of splashing and happy shrieking—the sound of the water lapping against the shore and the cracking sound of the beach stones shifting under people's feet.

Miranda slipped her arm through his, moving close to his body. 'Here?' she said.

'Here.' Leandro waited for the closure she'd spoken of but all he felt was the ache. The ache of loss, the noose of guilt that choked him so he could barely breathe. He could see his mother's face. The horror. The fear. The dread. He could see the ice-creams dropping from her hands to the sun-warmed stones on the shore. Funny how he always remembered that moment in such incredible detail, as if a camera lens inside his head had zoomed in at close range. One of the cones had landed upside down, the other had landed sideways, and the scoop of chocolate ice-cream had slid down the surface of a dark blue stone.

He could still see it melting there.

He could hear the shouts and cries. He could feel the confusion and the panic. It roared in his ears like he was hearing everything through a distorting vacuum. He could hear the shrieking sirens. He could see the flashes as police cars and an ambulance came screaming down the esplanade.

If only the ocean could talk. If only it could tell what it had witnessed all those years ago. What secrets were hidden below that deep blue vault?

'Are you okay?' Miranda's soft voice brought him back to the present.

Leandro put his arm around her shoulders and

brought her close to his side as they stood looking at the vastness of the ocean. 'My father used to come down here every day,' he said after a moment or two of silence. 'He would walk the length of the beach calling out for her. Every morning and every afternoon and every night. Sometimes I would go with him when I wasn't at school. I don't know if he kept doing it after Mum and I left. Probably.'

She slipped her arm around his waist and leaned her head against his upper arm, as she couldn't quite reach his shoulder. She didn't say anything but he felt her emotional support. It was a new feeling for him, having someone close enough to understand the heart-break of his past.

'I left a part of myself here that day and I can't get it back,' he said after another little silence.

Miranda turned to look up at him with tears shining in her eyes. 'You will get it back. You just have to stop blaming yourself.'

Easier said than done, Leandro thought as they walked back the way they had come.

CHAPTER EIGHT

A COUPLE OF days later, Miranda had finished packing up the last of the paintings ready for the shipping people to collect when she got a phone call from Jaz. Miranda gave her a quick rundown on Leandro's tragic background.

'Gosh, that's so sad,' Jaz said. 'I thought he was a bit distant because of his dad being a drunk. I didn't realise there was more to it than that.'

'Yes, I did too, but I think it's good he's finally talking about it,' Miranda said. 'He even took me to the place on the beach where his sister went missing. I was hoping it would give him some closure but I know he still blames himself. Maybe he always will.'

'Understandable, really,' Jaz said. 'So how are you two getting along?'

Miranda was glad she wasn't using the video-call option on her phone. 'Fine. I've sent off the paintings. Now we're sorting through his father's antiques. Some of them are amazing. His dad might have had a drinking problem but he sure knew how to track down a treasure or two.'

'Has Leandro made a move on you yet?'

Miranda thought of the moves Leandro had made on her last night and that morning. Achingly tender moves, on account of her soreness. It had made it harder to keep her emotions in check. He was so thoughtful and caring; how could she not begin to imagine them having a life together? 'You have a one-track mind,' she said. 'Did you get the dress done?'

'Yep. I'm working on a design for Holly as we speak,' Jaz said. 'Now, tell me all about it.'

Miranda frowned. 'All about what?'

'What you and Leandro have been getting up to apart from sorting out dusty old antiques and paintings.'

'We're not getting up to anything.'

'Hey, this is me—your best friend—you're talking to,' Jaz said. 'We've known each other since we were eight years old. You would've at least hugged him. You wouldn't be able to help yourself after he told you about his little sister. Am I right, Miss "Compassion and Tears at the Drop of a Hat" Ravensdale?'

'Anyone would do the same,' Miranda said. 'It doesn't mean I'm sleeping with him.'

'Aha!' Jaz said. 'Methinks more than a hug. A kiss, perhaps?'

Miranda knew it would be pointless denying it. Jaz was too astute to be fobbed off. 'We kissed and…stuff.'

'Stuff?'

'It's not serious,' she said. 'It's just a thing.'

'A thing?'

'A fling…sort of, but I hate that word, as it sounds so shallow.'

'Seriously?' Jaz said. 'You're *sleeping* with Leandro?'

Miranda frowned at the incredulity in her friend's tone. 'Isn't that what you thought I was doing?'

'You're actually doing the deed with Leandro Allegretti?' Jaz said. 'Oh. My. God. I think I'm going to pass out with shock.'

'It's just sex,' Miranda said. 'It's not as if we're dating or anything.'

'But what about Mark?' Jaz said. 'I thought you said there was never going to be another—'

'I'm not breaking my promise to Mark,' she said. 'Not really.'

'Listen, I never thought much of your promise in the first place,' Jaz said. 'Mark was nice and all, and it was awful that he died, but Leandro? *Seriously?* He's ten years older than you.'

'So?' Miranda shot back. 'Jake was ten years older than you when you had that silly little crush on him when you were sixteen.'

There was a tight little silence.

Miranda knew she shouldn't have thrown Jaz's crush on her brother in her face. She knew how much it upset Jaz to have been so madly infatuated with Jake back then. Even though Jaz had never told her what had actually happened in her brother's bedroom that night, it had obviously been something she wanted to forget. 'I'm sorry,' she said. 'That was mean of me.'

'Are you in love with him?' Jaz said.

'No.'

'Sure?'

The thing was, Miranda *wasn't* sure. She had always cared about Leandro. He was part of the family, a constant in her childhood, someone she had always respected and admired. She had loved him like a brother. Now her feelings for him were different. More mature. More adult.

But *in* love?

Or was it because of the amazing sex? She had read somewhere that good sex was deeply bonding. The more orgasms you had with a lover, the more you bonded with them. She wouldn't be the first woman to mistake physical compatibility for love.

'We're friends as well as lovers,' Miranda said.

'What's going to happen when he breaks it off?' Jaz said. 'Will you still be friends?'

'Of course,' Miranda said. 'Why wouldn't we be?'

'What if you want more?'

Miranda had already starting day-dreaming them as a couple—as a permanent couple. Becoming engaged. Getting married. Going through life as a team, building a future together. Having children and raising them in a household with love and security—all the things he had missed out on.

But then there was her promise to Mark to consider. She would have to tell Mark's parents she was ready to move on with her life. She would have to stop feeling guilty for being alive when Mark was not. She would have to confront the fact that maybe she hadn't loved Mark the way she had thought. That they hadn't been soul mates but just two teenagers who had dated. 'I don't want more.'

'What if Leandro does?' Jaz asked.

'He doesn't,' she said. 'He's not the commitment type.'

'That could change.'

'It won't,' she said. 'He only ever dates a woman for a month or two.'

'So you're his Miss October.'

Miranda didn't care for her friend's blunt summation of the situation. But that was Jaz. She didn't sugar-coat anything—she doused it in bitter aloes. 'Stop worrying about me,' Miranda said. 'I know what I'm doing. But I'd appreciate it if you didn't let it slip to my brothers, okay?'

'Fine,' Jaz said. 'I only ever speak to one of your brothers, in any case. But are you going to tell Mark's parents?'

Miranda bit down on her lip as she thought about that poignant ICU bedside scene seven years ago. Her promise to Mark had comforted his parents. They still got comfort from having her call on them, spending time with them on Mark's birthday and the anniversary of his death. How could she tell them she was falling in love with someone else? It would shatter them all over again. It would be better to let this short phase in her life come and go without comment. She couldn't bear to hurt them when they had been so loving and kind towards her. They needed her. She saw the way their faces lit up every time she called in. She lifted their spirits. She gave them a break from the depressing emptiness of their life without their son. 'Why would I tell them?' Miranda said.

'What if someone sees you with Leandro?' Jaz said. 'He's been photographed in the press before. He's one of London's most eligible bachelors. You and him being linked would be big news, especially right now, with your dad's stuff doing the rounds. Everyone wants to know what the scandalous Ravensdales are up to.'

Miranda groaned. 'Did you have to remind me?'

'Sorry, but you guys are seriously hot property just now,' Jaz said. 'Even I'm being targeted on account of being an adjunct to the family.'

'Really?'

'Yeah. I'm thinking I might meet up with this Kat chick,' Jaz said. 'She sounds kind of cool.'

'Why do you think that?' Miranda said, feeling a sharp sting of betrayal deep in her gut.

'I like her ballsy attitude,' Jaz said. 'She's not going to be told what to do no matter how much money your family's hot-shot lawyer, Flynn Carlyon, waves under her nose.'

Miranda couldn't bear the thought of Jaz kicking goals for the opposition. Jaz was an honorary family member. She was the sister she had always longed for. Ever since Jaz's mother had dropped her off for an access visit at Ravensdene and never returned, Miranda and Jaz had been a solid team. When the mean girls had bullied Miranda at boarding school, Jaz had stepped up and dealt with them. Jaz had been there for her when Mark had got sick and had been there for her when he died. Jaz had been everything and more that a blood sister would be. The prospect of her becoming friendly with Miranda's father's love child was unthinkable. Unpalatable. Unbearable. 'Well, I *don't* want to meet her,' she said. 'I can't think of anything worse.'

'I can,' Jaz said. 'Leandro lost his little sister and here you are pushing away what you've always wanted. It doesn't make sense. The least you could do is make the first move. Be the bigger person and all that.'

Miranda frowned. 'I don't need a sister. Why would I? I have you.'

'But we're not blood sisters,' Jaz said. 'You shouldn't turn your back on blood. Only crazy people do that.'

Miranda knew there was a wealth of hurt in Jaz's words. Jaz put on a brash don't-mess-with-me front but deep down she was still that little bewildered eight-year-old girl who had been dropped off at the big mansion in Buckinghamshire and had watched as her mother drove away from her down the long driveway into a future that didn't include her. Miranda had heard Jaz cry herself to sleep for weeks. It had been years before Jaz had told her some of the things her mother had subjected her to: being left in the care of strangers while her mother had turned tricks to feed her drug habit; being punished for things no child should ever be punished for. Jaz had suffered horrendous neglect because her mother had been too busy, or too manic, or off her face with drugs, to care about her welfare.

But Miranda didn't want to meet the result of her father's infidelity to her mother. If she met Katherine Winwood she would be betraying her mother. Elisabetta was devastated by Richard's behaviour. How

could she not be when at the time of his affair with
Kat's mother he had been reconciling with her?

Miranda had spent most of her life trying to please
her mother, living up to the unreachable standards of
her beautiful, talented and extroverted mother. This
was one way to get the relationship with her mother
she had yearned for. If she met with her father's love
child it would undo everything she had worked so hard
to achieve.

Besides, Kat Winwood hadn't expressed any desire
to meet her half-siblings. She was apparently doing her
level best to avoid all contact with the Ravensdales.

Long may it continue, Miranda thought.

Leandro had just finished talking on the phone to an
estate agent when Miranda came into the study. 'I think
I've got a buyer for the villa,' he said, putting his phone
down on the desk. 'Hey, what's wrong?'

She came and perched on the edge of the walnut
desk, kicking one of her slim ankles back and forth, her
mouth pushed forward in a pout. 'Jaz thinks I should
meet Katherine Winwood. She thinks I should make
the first move.'

He took her nearest hand and stroked the back of
it with his thumb. 'I think that would be a really good
thing to do,' he said.

'But what about Mum?' she said, frowning. 'She'll
think I'm betraying her if I become best buddies with
her husband's love child. God, this is such a mess. Why
can't I have normal parents?'

'Your mother will have to deal with it,' Leandro said. 'None of this is Kat's fault, remember.'

Miranda let out a long breath. 'I know, but I hate how Dad wants everything to be smoothed over as if he didn't do anything wrong. He doesn't just want his cake and eat it too, he wants to decorate it and hand out pieces to everyone as well.'

'People do wrong stuff all the time,' Leandro said. 'There comes a time when you have to forgive them for it and move on. For everyone's sake.'

She brought her gaze back to his. 'Is that what you're doing? Forgiving yourself as well as your father?'

Am I? Leandro thought. Was it time to accept some things were outside his control and always had been? He hadn't been able to protect his sister. He hadn't been able to save his parents' marriage. He hadn't been able to protect his father from self-destructing. He hadn't come home in time to say goodbye to his father, but he was here now, surrounded by the things his father had treasured. Being here in the place where his father had spent so many lonely years had given Leandro a greater sense of who his father was. Vittorio Allegretti hadn't planned to live alone. He hadn't planned to drink himself into an early grave. He had once been a young man full of enthusiasm for life, and then life had thrown him things that had made him stumble and fall and he simply hadn't been able to get back up again. 'Maybe a little,' Leandro said.

A little silence passed.

Miranda looked down at their joined hands. 'I hope

you don't mind, but I kind of told Jaz we're seeing each other...'

Leandro frowned. 'Kind of?'

She met his gaze, her cheeks a faint shade of pink. 'It's impossible to keep anything a secret from Jaz. She knows me too well. She put two and two together and... well... I confessed we're having a thing.'

Is that what we're having? he thought. *A thing?* Why did it feel much more than that? It didn't feel like any other relationship he'd had in the past. It felt closer. More meaningful. More intimate. He felt like a different person when he was with her. He felt like a whole person, not someone who had compartmentalised himself into tidy little boxes that didn't intersect.

Why did it make him feel empty inside at the thought of bringing their 'thing' to an end?

'I don't like calling it a fling,' Miranda continued. 'And given what my father did I absolutely loathe the word affair. It sounds so...so tawdry.'

Leandro didn't like the words either. He didn't like using the word 'affair' or 'fling' to describe what he was experiencing with Miranda. As far as he was concerned, there was nothing tawdry or illicit about his involvement with her. He had always had a relationship with her—a friendship that was distant but polite. He had always cared about her because she was a sweet girl who was a part of the family he adored. Even her parents—for all their foibles—were very dear to him. Miranda's brothers were his best mates. He didn't want his involvement with her to jeopardise the long-standing mateship he valued so much.

But defining what he had with her now was complicated. The more time he spent with her, the more he wanted. Her gentle and compassionate nature was soothing to be around. But she deserved to have all the things girls her age wanted. He couldn't commit to that sort of relationship. It wouldn't be fair to her to allow her to think he could. He had been honest with her. Allowing their involvement to go on when they returned to England would be offering her false hope. Postponing the inevitable. It would make it harder to let go if he held on too long.

Once her family found out they were seeing each other, there would be pressure from them to take things to the next level. There would be pressure from the public because everyone loved a celebrity romance. The press had already taken an avid interest in Julius's engagement to Holly. What would they do with the news of Leandro and Miranda's involvement?

'Miranda...' He gave her hand a gentle squeeze. 'I know I've said this before, but you do realise we can't continue this when we go back home, don't you?'

She didn't quite meet his gaze. 'Are you worried what Julius and Jake will say?'

Leandro raised her chin so her eyes met his. 'It's not about what your brothers think. It's about me. About what I can and can't give.'

'But you'd make a wonderful partner,' she said with an earnest expression. 'I know you would. You're so caring and kind and considerate. How can you think you wouldn't be happy in a long-term relationship?'

'But you don't want a long-term relationship,' he said, watching her closely.

Her eyes went back to his chin as if that was the most fascinating part of his anatomy. 'I wasn't talking about me per se… It's just I think you'd be a great person for someone to spend the rest of their life with. To have a family with and stuff.'

He let out a heavy sigh. 'It's not what I want.'

She pressed her lips together for a beat or two of silence. 'I suppose you think I've fallen madly in love with you.'

'Have you?'

Her eyes still didn't quite make the full distance to his. 'That would be rather fickle of me, given this time last week I was in love with Mark.'

Leandro brushed her cheek with his fingertip. 'You're twenty-three—still a baby. You'll fall in love with dozens of men before you settle down.' The thought of her with someone else made his chest ache. What if they didn't treat her right? She was an incredibly sensitive person. She could so easily be taken advantage of. She was always over-adapting to accommodate other people's needs and expectations. Even the fact that she'd settled for his 'thing' with her was evidence of how easily she could be exploited.

Not that he was exploiting her…or was he? He had been as honest as he could be. He hadn't given her any promises he couldn't keep. She had accepted the terms and yet… How could he know for sure what she had invested in their relationship? She acted like a woman in love, but then anyone looking in from the outside would think he was madly in love with her. Being physically intimate with someone blurred the boundaries. Was it lust or love that motivated her to be with him?

How could he tell the difference?

His own feelings he left in the file inside his head labelled 'Do Not Open'. It served no purpose to think about the feelings he had for Miranda. He would have to let her go. He couldn't hold her to him indefinitely. Over the years he had taught himself not to think of the things he wanted—the things most people wanted. He had almost convinced himself he was happy living the single-and-loving-it life. Almost.

Miranda slipped off the desk and smoothed her hands down her jeans. 'I should leave you to get on with your work…'

Leandro captured her hand and brought her close to his body, watching as her pupils flared as his head came down. 'Work can wait,' he said and pressed his mouth to hers.

Desire rose hot and strong in him as her mouth flowered open beneath his. He stroked his tongue against hers, a shudder of pleasure rocketing through him when her tongue came back at him in shy little darts and dives. He spread his hands through her hair, cupping her head so he could deepen the kiss, savouring the sweet, hot passion of her.

Her small dainty frame was pressed tightly against him, her mouth clamped to his as her fingers stroked through his hair. Her touch sent hot wires of need through his body. The slightest movement of her fingers made the blood surge in his veins.

He wondered if he would ever forget her touch. He wondered if he would ever forget her taste. Or the way she felt in his arms, like she belonged there and nowhere else. He wondered how he would be able to make love to someone else without making comparisons. Right now he couldn't envisage ever making love to anyone else. How could someone else's touch make his flesh tingle all over? How could someone else's kiss stoke a fire so consuming inside him he felt it in every cell of his body?

'Make love to me here,' Miranda said, whisper-soft, against his mouth.

Leandro didn't need a second invitation. He was fighting for control as it was. Every office fantasy he had ever had was coming to life in his arms. Miranda was working her way down his body, her hands shaping him through the fabric of his jeans, then unzipping him and going in search of him. The smooth, cool grasp of her fingers around his swollen heat made him stifle an animalistic groan. She read his body like a secret code-breaker, stroking him, caressing him, taking him to the brink, before pulling back so he could snatch in another breath. 'Let's even this up a bit,' he said and started on her clothes.

She gave a soft little gasp as he uncovered her breasts. He brought his mouth to each tightly budded nipple, rolling his tongue around each one. He drew on each nipple with careful suction, delighting in the way she responded with breathless sounds of delight. He moved to the underside of her breast where he knew she was most sensitive. He trailed his tongue over the creamy perfection of her flesh, his groin hard with want as he felt her shudder with reaction.

Miranda wriggled her jeans down to her ankles but he didn't give her time to step out of them. Leandro didn't step out of his either. He eased her back against the desk, deftly sourcing a condom before he entered her with a deep, primal groan of satisfaction. Her tight little body gripped him, milking him with every thrusting movement he made within her. He had to force himself to slow down in case he hurt her or went off early. But she was with him all the way, urging him on with panting cries. He worked a hand between their hard-pressed bodies to give her the extra stimulation she needed. It didn't take much. She was so wet and swollen he barely stroked her before she came hard around him, making it impossible for him to hold on any longer.

He shuddered, quaked, emptied. Then he held still while the afterglow passed through him like the gentle suck and hiss of a wave.

Miranda's legs were still wrapped around him as she propped herself on her elbows to look at him, her features flushed pink with pleasure, a playful smile curving her lips. 'Should I have told you first I was a desk virgin?'

He pressed a kiss to the exposed skin of her belly, letting his stubble lightly graze her flesh. 'I would never have guessed.'

She shivered as he went lower. 'I haven't done it outdoors either.'

Leandro thought of the timeframe on their relation-

ship with a jarring sense of panic. There wasn't time
to do all the things he wanted to do with her. In a matter of days they would go back to being friends. There
would be no making love under the stars. No making
love on a remote beach or in a private pool. No making
love on a picnic rug under a shady tree in a secluded
spot. He hadn't done those things with anyone else for
years. Some of those things he had never done. How
had he let his life get so boring and mundane?

The sound of his phone ringing where it was lying
on the desk confirmed how much he had hemmed himself in with work. It rang day and night. He had forty
emails to sort through, ten text messages to respond
to and fifteen calls to make before he missed the time
zone differences.

Miranda reached for his phone to hand it to him and
then blushed as she glanced at the screen. 'It's Jake,'
she said in a shocked whisper, as if her brother could
hear without the phone even being answered.

Leandro took the phone off her, turned it to silent
and put it back on the desk. 'I'll call him later.'

She slipped off the desk and pulled up her jeans.
Her teeth were savaging her bottom lip, her eyes avoiding all contact with his as she went in search of her
top and bra.

He pulled up his own jeans before he took her by
the hand and drew her close. 'There's no need to feel
ashamed of what we're doing.'

Miranda glanced at him briefly before lowering
her gaze to his chin. 'I'm not… It's just that… I don't
know…' She slipped out of his hold and ran a hand

through her hair like a wide-toothed comb. 'What if he finds out?'

'He won't unless you tell him.'

She gave him a worried glance. 'But what if Jaz tells him?'

Leandro gave her a wry look. 'Jaz talking to Jake? You seriously think that's going to happen any time soon?'

She chewed at her lip again, hugging her arms around her body. 'Will you tell him or Julius?'

That was the other file inside Leandro's head—the 'Too Hard' file. The conversation with her brothers about his thing with Miranda wasn't something he was looking forward to. It would have to happen at some point. He couldn't hope to keep it a secret for ever and nor would he want to in case they heard about it later via someone else. He suspected Jake and Julius would guess as soon as they saw him and Miranda together at a Ravensdale gathering.

Like at Julius and Holly's wedding next month. He couldn't get out of going as he was one of the grooms-men, along with Jake, who was best man. Miranda was one of the bridesmaids. Maybe he would have to decline all future invitations. But then that would only increase speculation. 'They'll have to know eventually,' he said. 'I've kept enough secrets from them as it is.'

Her brow was still puckered with a frown. 'I know, but…'

Leandro rubbed his hands up and down her upper arms in a soothing motion. 'But you're worried what they'll think? You don't need to be. I reckon they'll be happy you're finally moving on with your life.'

The trouble was she would be moving on with her life with *someone else*, he thought with another sharp dart of pain in his gut. He would have to stand to one side as she walked up the aisle to some other guy. He would have to pretend it didn't matter because it *shouldn't* matter.

Miranda lifted her toffee-brown gaze to his. 'But what about you?' she said. 'Will you move on with yours?'

Leandro gave her a crooked smile. 'I already have. You've helped me with that.'

'I have?'

'Sure you have,' he said. 'You've helped me understand my father a little better.'

She touched a gentle hand to his face. 'I'm sure he loved you. How could he not?'

Leandro captured her hand and pressed a kiss to the middle of her palm. 'I'd better call your brother back. You want to hang around and say hi to him?'

Her eyes widened in alarm as she started to back away. 'Not right now... I—I think I'll have to take a bath.'

'Leave some hot water for me, okay?'

She nodded and scampered out of the room.

Leandro let out a breath and pressed the call button on his phone. 'Jake, sorry I was busy with something when you called.'

'So, what's this about you doing my little sister?' Jake said.

Leandro felt a chill tighten his skin. 'Where'd you hear that?'

'Joke, man,' Jake laughed.

'Right…'

'You okay?'

'Sure,' Leandro said. 'Been busy sorting out my father's stuff. Now, about this Braystone account—'

'So have you introduced Miranda to any hot French or Italian guys over there?' Jake said.

'No,' he said, trying not to clench his jaw. 'Not yet.'

'Not that it'd work,' Jake said. 'But it's worth a try.'

'I'm sure when she's ready to date again she will,' Leandro said. 'You can't force people into doing stuff until they're ready emotionally. You and Julius shouldn't be giving her such a hard time about it. It's probably why she's been pushing back for all this time. Give her the space to recognise what she needs and stop lecturing her. She's not a fool.'

'Whoa there, buddy,' Jake said. 'No need to take my head off.'

'I'm just saying you need to back off a little, okay?'

'Okey dokey,' Jake said. 'Point taken. Now, about this Braystone account. It's a humdinger of a puzzle, isn't it?'

Leandro mentally gave a deep sigh of relief. *Work.* Now that was something he was comfortable talking about.

CHAPTER NINE

THERE WERE ONLY two days left before Miranda was to fly back to London. How had the last few days gone so quickly? It seemed like yesterday when she had arrived and walked into the villa with Leandro to all the dusts and secrets inside. Now the villa was all but empty apart from the kitchen, the bedroom they'd been sharing and Rosie's room. He hadn't done anything about that yet and Miranda didn't want to push him. She knew he would do it when he was ready. He had a couple more days here after she left before he flew on to Geneva for a meeting over the big account he was working on for Jake.

Miranda looked at the date on the flight itinerary on her phone with a sinking feeling. Forty-eight hours and it would all be over. She and Leandro would go back to being friends. Platonic friends. They would no longer touch. No longer kiss. No longer make love. They would move on with their lives as if nothing had happened. She would have to interact with him at Julius and Holly's wedding, maybe even dance with him and pretend they were as they had been before—distant friends. How was she going to do it? Wouldn't everyone see the chemistry they activated in each other? She didn't think she would be able to hide her emotions or her response to his presence. She had no control over how he made her feel. He had only to look at her and she felt her body tremble with need.

He wasn't in love with her. She was almost sure of it. He certainly acted like it but he had never said the words. Every kiss, every caress, every time he made love to her, she wanted to believe he was doing it out of love instead of lust. But if he loved her why hadn't he changed his mind about the time frame of their involvement? He hadn't even mentioned it since the evening in his office. Had it been her imagination or had he been distancing himself since that night? She knew he was worried about the account he was working on. There were lawyers involved and a court hearing scheduled. Every spare minute when he wasn't sorting out his father's stuff he worked on his laptop with a deep frown etched on his forehead. She had tried to give him the space he needed to work in peace, even though it had been more than tempting to interrupt him and have him make love to her the way he had before.

But at night when he finally came to bed he would reach for her. His arms would go around her; his mouth, hands and deliciously male body would pleasure her until she was tingling from head to foot. She would sometimes wake and see him lying on his side looking at her, one of his hands idly stroking her arm or the back of her hand.

How could that just be lust?

The date blurred in front of Miranda's vision. How could she leave without telling him how she felt? But how could she tell him when he had warned her from the start about moving the goal posts? She was supposed to be an adult about this. Do what everyone else her age did—have flings and 'things' with no strings. She wasn't supposed to fall in love. Not with Leandro. He had always been so honest with her. He hadn't made any promises or misled her in any way. She knew what she had been signing up for and yet she had broken the first rule.

The love she felt for him felt completely different from what she had felt for Mark. More adult. More mature. She loved him with her body and her mind. She couldn't separate the two, which was part of the problem. She couldn't separate her desire for him from her love of him. They were so deeply, inextricably entwined, like two parts of a whole.

Something about that date on her phone calendar began to niggle at the back of her mind.... She was as regular as clockwork. She should have had her period two days ago. She couldn't be pregnant...could she? But they had used protection. Condoms were fairly reliable, weren't they? She wasn't on the pill because she hadn't needed to be.

Surely it was too early to be panicking? Periods could be disrupted by stress and travel—not that hers had ever been disrupted before. They were annoyingly, persistently regular. She could set her watch by when the tell-tale cramps would start.

Miranda put a hand on her abdomen. Could it be

possible? Could Leandro and her have made a tiny baby? The thought of having her very own baby made the membrane around her heart tighten. How could she have thought she could go through life without experiencing motherhood? Of course she wanted a baby. She wanted to be a mother more than anything. She wanted to be a wife, but not just anyone's wife. She wanted to be Leandro's wife. How could she live the rest of her life without him beside her? He was everything to her. He had shown her what she was capable of feeling as a woman. He had unlocked her frozen heart. He had awakened the needs she had suppressed. He was The One. The Only One. How could she not have realised that before now? But maybe a part of her had always been a little bit in love with him.

Would the prospect of having a baby change his mind about them having a future together?

Miranda gnawed at her lip. It would be best to make sure she was actually pregnant first. She would have to slip out and get a test kit and take it from there. There was no point in mentioning it until she was absolutely sure. Her mind ran with a spinning loop of worry. How would he take it if the test was positive? She couldn't imagine how she was going to find the courage to tell him. *'Hey, guess what? We made a baby.'* Like that was going to go down well. How would she explain it to her family? Or Mark's family?

Leandro was tied up with the gardening team who were sorting out the garden in preparation for selling the villa. Miranda told him she was going to do some shopping for dinner, which was fortunately partially true. She was the world's worst liar and didn't want to raise his suspicions. Luckily he was preoccupied with the gardeners, as he simply kissed her on the forehead before turning back to speak to the head gardener.

Inside the pharmacy there were two young mothers. One was buying nappies; the other was looking at nursing aids. Their babies were under six months old. Miranda couldn't stop staring at them sleeping in their prams. In a few months' time she would have one just like them. Would it be a girl or a boy? Would he or she look like her or Leandro or a combination of them both? One of the babies opened its mouth and gave a wide yawn, its little starfish hands opening and closing against the soft blue bunny blanket it was snuggly wrapped in.

Miranda felt a groundswell of emotion sweep through her. How had she managed to convince herself she didn't want to be a mother? She wanted to be just like these young mothers—shopping with their babies, doing all the things mothers do. Taking care of their little family, loving them, nurturing them, watching them grow and mature. Taking the good with the bad, the triumphs with the tragedies, because that was what made a full and authentic life.

Miranda came home with three testing kits and quickly took them upstairs to the bathroom off her suite. Not that she had slept another night in her suite. She had spent every night with Leandro in his. Could that mean he wanted her to be in his life more permanently? Hope lifted in her chest but then it deflated like a pricked balloon. She was in his room because the furniture had been packed up in hers. It was a convenience thing, not an emotional one.

Her heart was in her throat as she waited for the test to work. She blinked when the results came through. *Negative?* How could it possibly be negative? She snatched up the packaging and reread the instructions. Maybe she hadn't followed the directions. No. She'd done exactly what she was supposed to do. Maybe it was too early to tell. She was only a couple of days past her period time. Maybe she didn't have strong enough hormonal activity yet.

But she *felt* pregnant.

Or was it the hope of it she was feeling? The hope of a new life growing inside her—a life that would bond her and Leandro together for ever. A little baby boy or girl like those she had seen in the pharmacy. The little baby who would be the first child of the family she had always wanted.

Miranda did another test and another one. Each one came up negative. The disappointment was worse each time. She held up the first test for another look and her heart stopped like it had been struck with a thick plank when she saw Leandro reflected in the mirror in front of her.

'What are you doing up here?' he said. 'You know you can use my bathroom.'

She turned to face him, hiding the test stick behind her back. 'Erm…nothing…'

His eyes went to the pile of packaging on the marble top near the basin to the right of her. Miranda's heart felt like it was going to pound its way out of her chest.

She could feel it hammering against her breastbone as Leandro stepped into the bathroom. It wasn't a tiny bathroom by any means but now it felt like a shoebox. She watched in scalp-tingling dread as he picked up one of the packages.

He turned and looked at her with a deep frown. 'What's going on?'

Miranda licked her tinder-dry lips. 'I thought I was pregnant, but I'm not, so you don't have to panic. I did a test. Three times. There were all negative.' Tears were close. She could feel them building up behind her eyes. Stinging, burning. Threatening to spill over.

'Pregnant?' His voice sounded hoarse.

'Yes, but it's all good,' she said, swallowing a knotty lump of emotion. 'You don't have to change your brand of condoms. They've done the job.'

His frown was so tight his brows were joined over the bridge of his nose. 'Why didn't you tell me earlier?'

'I only just realised I was late,' Miranda said. 'I'm never late. I wanted to make sure before I told you. I didn't see the point in telling you if there was nothing to worry about. And there's nothing to worry about, so you don't have to worry.'

He put the package down and raked a hand through his hair with a hand that wasn't steady. His face was a strange colour. Not his usual olive tan but blanched, ashen. 'So…you weren't going to tell me unless it was positive?'

'No.'

He studied her for a moment. 'Are you relieved it was negative?'

'I...' Miranda couldn't do it. She couldn't tell another white lie. It was time to face up to what she had been avoiding for the last twelve days—for the last seven years. 'I'm bitterly disappointed,' she said. 'I want a baby. I want to be a mother. I want to have a family. I can't pretend I don't. I *ache* when I see mothers and babies. I ache so deep inside it takes my breath away. I can't do this any more, Leandro. I know you don't want what I want. I know you can't bear the thought of having a child in case you can't keep them safe. But I want to take that risk. I want to live my life and take all the risks it dishes up because locking myself away hasn't made me happy. It hasn't brought Mark back and it hasn't helped his parents move on. I'm ready to move on.' She took a deep breath and added, 'I want to move on with you.'

A flicker of pain passed over his face. 'I can't. I told you before. I can't.'

Miranda's heart sank. 'Are you saying you don't love me?'

His jaw worked for a moment. 'I'm saying I can't give you what you want.'

Miranda fought back tears. 'You love me. I know you do. I see it every time you look at me. I feel it every time you touch me. We belong together. You know we do.'

He turned to grip the edges of the marble counter, his back turned towards her as if he couldn't bear to look at her. Self-doubt suddenly assailed her. Could she be wrong? Could she have got it horribly wrong? Maybe he didn't love her. Maybe all this had been for him was a 'thing'. Maybe she was just another one of his casual flings that didn't mean anything.

'Leandro?'

He pushed himself away from the counter and turned to look at her, his expression taut, his posture stiff as if every muscle was being drawn back inside his body. 'It was wrong of me to get involved with you like this. I'm not the right person for you. I'm not the right person for anybody.'

'That's not true,' Miranda said. 'You're letting the past dictate your future. That's what I was doing. For the last seven years I've been living in the past. Clinging to the past because I was too frightened of loving someone and losing them. I can't live like that any more. I'm not afraid to love. I love you. I think I probably always have loved you. Maybe not quite as intensely as I do now, but the first time you touched me it changed something. It changed me. You changed me.'

'You're in love with the idea of love,' Leandro said. 'You always have been. That's why you latched onto Mark the way you did. You're doing it now to me. You like to be needed. You like to fix things for people. You couldn't fix things for Mark so you gave him the rest of your life. You can't fix me, Miranda. You can't make me into something I'm not. And I sure as hell don't want you to give me the rest of your life so I can ruin it like I've ruined everyone else's.'

Miranda took a painful breath. 'What if that test had been positive?' she said. 'What would you have done then?'

He looked at her with his mouth tightly set. 'I would have respected your decision either way.'

But he would have hated it, she thought. He would have hated her for putting him through it for she could never have made the decision to terminate. Not when she wanted a baby more than anything. Why had it taken her this long to see the lie she had been living? Or had she lived like that because everyone had kept telling her what she should do for so long, she had dug her heels in without stopping to reflect on what she was actually giving up? But if Leandro couldn't give her what she wanted then there was no point in pretending and hoping he would some day change his mind.

She was done with pretending.

She had to be true to herself, to her dreams and hopes. She loved Leandro, but if he couldn't love her back then she would accept it, even though it would break her heart.

But life was full of heart-breaking moments.

It was what life was all about: you lived, you learned, you hurt, you healed, you hurt and healed all over again.

'I know you warned me about changing the rules,' Miranda said. 'But I couldn't control my feelings. Not the way you seem to be able to do. I want to be with you. I can't imagine being with anyone else. I know we only have two days left, in any case, but it would be wrong of me—wrong *for* me—to stay another minute knowing you can't love me the way I want and need to be loved.'

Nothing showed in his expression to suggest that

he was even remotely upset by her announcement. She could have been one of the gardeners outside telling him she had finished for the day. 'If you feel you must leave now, then fine,' he said. 'I'll bring your flight forward.'

Do you need any further confirmation than that? Miranda thought. He couldn't wait to get rid of her. Why wasn't he reaching for her and saying, *don't be silly, ma petite, let's talk about this*? Why wasn't he holding her close and resting his chin on the top of her head the way he so often did that made her feel so treasured and so safe? Why wasn't he saying he had made a mistake and that *of course* he loved her? How he had *always* loved her and wanted the same things she wanted. Why was he standing there as if she was a virtual stranger instead of the lover he had been so intimately tender and passionate with only hours earlier?

Because he doesn't love you.

'If you don't mind, I'll make my own way to the airport,' Miranda said. 'I hate goodbyes.'

'Fine,' he said and pulled out his phone. 'I'll order a cab.'

Miranda didn't waste time unpacking her bag when she got home to her flat. She went to her wardrobe and pulled out the drawer that contained Mark's football jersey. She unwrapped it from the tissue paper she kept it in and held it up to her face but all she could smell was the lavender sachet she had put in the drawer beside it. She gently folded the jersey and put it in a cardboard carrier bag.

Mark's parents greeted her warmly when she arrived at their house a short time later. She hugged them back and then handed them the carrier bag. 'I've been holding onto this for too long,' she said. 'It belongs here with you.'

Mark's mother, Susanne, opened the bag and promptly burst into tears as she took out Mark's jersey and pressed it to her chest. Mark's father, James, put a comforting arm around his wife's shoulders while he fought back his own tears.

'I'm not sure if I've helped or hindered your grieving of Mark,' Miranda said. 'But I think it's time I moved on with my life.'

Susanne enveloped Miranda in a warm motherly hug. 'You helped,' she said. 'I don't know what we would've done without you, especially in the early days. But you're right. It's time to move on. For all of us.'

James stepped forward for his hug. 'You've been marvellous,' he said. 'I'm not sure Mark would've been as loyal if things had been different. Susanne and I are looking into fostering kids in crisis. We're ready now to be parents again, even if it's only in temporary bursts.'

Miranda smiled through her tears. 'Wow, that's amazing. You'll be fantastic at fostering. You're wonderful parents. Mark was so lucky to have you. *I've* been lucky to have you.'

'You'll still have us,' Susanne said, hugging Miranda again. 'You'll always have us. We'll always be here for you.'

Miranda waved to them as she left, wondering if she would ever see them again, but then decided she would.

They would always have a special place in her life, just as Mark would.

Leandro couldn't put it off any longer. He had to pack up Rosie's room. Everything else had been seen to: the paintings had gone; the antiques were sold—apart from a few things he couldn't bear to part with. His father's walnut desk and the brass carriage clock that sat on the bookshelves nearby and gave that soothing tick-tock of time passing steadily by. The villa was an empty shell now everything had been taken away. The floors and corridors echoed as he walked along them. The rooms were like cold caves.

All except for Rosie's room.

He opened the door and the memories hit him like a tidal wave...not of Rosie so much, but of Miranda standing in there with him. Of her standing with him, supporting him, understanding him. Loving him.

His eyes went to Flopsy. The silly rabbit had fallen over again. Leandro walked over and picked the toy up but, instead of putting it back against the pillows, he hugged it against his chest where a knot of tightly bound emotion was unravelling.

He had let Miranda leave.

How could he have done that when she was the only one he wanted to be with? She was the only one who understood his grief. The only one who understood how hard it was to move on from the past.

But at least she'd had the courage to do so.

He had baulked at it.

Seeing those pregnancy tests on the bathroom counter had thrown him. It had thrown him back to the past where he hadn't been careful enough, not diligent enough, to protect his little sister.

But Miranda was right. It was time to move on. He hadn't done anything deliberately. He had been a child—a small, innocent child.

He finally understood why his father had left him his most treasured possessions. His dad hadn't been able to move on from the past but he had known Leandro would have the courage to do so.

He had the courage now. He had it in spades.

He was an adult now and he wanted the things most adults wanted. He wanted to love and be loved. He wanted to have a family. He wanted to build a future with someone who had the same values as he did.

Miranda was that person.

He loved her. He loved her with a love big enough to overcome the past. He loved her with a love that could withstand whatever life dished up. How could he have let her leave? Why had it taken him this long to see what was right before his eyes? Or had he known, always known, but shied away from it? Hadn't he felt it the first time they kissed? The way her mouth met his, the way her arms looped around his neck, the way her body pressed into his, the way she responded to him with such passion and generosity.

He had been a fool to let her go. He had hurt her and the very last thing he wanted to do was that. Her pregnancy scare had thrown him. Terrified him. Shocked him into an emotional stasis. He had locked down. He hadn't been able to process the enormity of his feelings. All the hopes and dreams he had been suppressing for all those years had hit him in the face when he'd seen that pregnancy test. It had been like a carrot being dangled in front of his nose: *this is what you could have if only you had the courage to take it.*

Speaking of carrots… Leandro smiled at the floppy-eared rabbit in his hands. 'I think I've just found the perfect home for you.'

Miranda was on her way out to her car to meet Jaz at the boutique when she saw a dark blue BMW pull up. Her heart gave a little leap when she saw a tall figure unfold from behind the wheel. Leandro was carrying something in a bag but she couldn't see what it was. She wondered if she had left something behind at the villa, as she had packed in rather a hurry. She didn't allow herself to think he was here for any other reason. Her hopes had been elevated before and look how that had turned out.

She opened the door before he pressed the buzzer. 'Hi. I thought you were going to Geneva?'

He smiled at her. An actual smile! Not a quarter-one. Not a half-one, but a full one. It totally transformed his face. It took years off him, made him look even more heart-stoppingly gorgeous than ever. 'I postponed the meeting,' he said. 'Is now a good time to talk?'

Miranda hoped Jaz wouldn't mind her being a few minutes late. Even if he was just returning a stray pair

MELANIE MILBURNE 183

of knickers it would be worth it to see him smile again. 'Sure,' she said. 'Come in.'

He stooped as he came inside and her belly gave a card-shuffling movement as she caught the citrus notes of his aftershave. She had to restrain herself from reaching out and touching him to make sure she wasn't imagining him there. *Why* was he here? He'd said he wanted to talk but that might be about how to keep the news of their 'thing' a secret from her family, especially with Julius' and Holly's wedding coming up. She didn't dare hope for anything more.

Miranda glanced at the bag in his hand. 'Did I leave something behind?'

He handed it to her. 'I want you to have this.'

Miranda opened the bag to find Flopsy the rabbit inside. She took him out and held him close to her thrumming chest. 'Why?'

'Because I want our first baby to have him,' Leandro said.

She blinked and then frowned, not sure she'd heard him correctly. 'But we're not pregnant. I told you, the tests were all negative. You don't have to worry. It was my mistake. I worked myself up into a panic over nothing.'

He stepped closer and held her by the upper arms, a gentle, protective touch that made her flesh shiver in delight. His dark brown eyes were meltingly warm, moist with banked-up emotion. 'I want you to marry me,' he said. 'I want you to have my babies. As many as you want. I love you. I don't think it's possible to love someone more than I love you.'

Miranda's heart was so full of love, joy and relief, she thought it would burst. Could this really be happening? Was he really proposing to her? '*Really?*' she said. 'Did you really just ask me to marry you?'

'Yes, really.'

'What made you change your mind?'

'When you left I kept telling myself it was for the best,' he said. 'I convinced myself it was better that way. I was annoyed with myself for crossing a boundary I'd always told myself I'd never cross. But when I finally worked up the courage to pack up Rosie's room it made me realise what I was forfeiting. I think that's why I was so shocked at seeing that pregnancy test. It was like being slammed over the head with the truth. The truth of what I really wanted all this time but wasn't game to admit. I *want* to risk loving you and our children. I can't promise to keep you and them safe, but I will do everything in my power to do so. No one can offer more than that.'

Miranda threw her arms around his neck, Flopsy getting caught up in the hug. 'I love you,' she said. 'I want to spend the rest of my life with you. I can't imagine being with anyone else.'

Leandro kissed her tenderly before holding her slightly aloft so he could look down at her. 'You know what's ironic about this? That night I returned Jake's call, I lectured him about hassling you all the time about moving on with your life. I told him all you needed was some space to sort it out for yourself. But then I realised that's what I needed. When you left I could finally see what I was throwing away. I didn't want to end up like my father, living alone and desperately lonely, with only liquor for comfort. He knew I would eventually get past the grief and guilt. That's why he left me what he loved most. He knew I would reclaim my life. I want to be with you while I do it, *ma petite*. No one else but you.'

Miranda wrapped her arms around his waist. 'I wonder what my brothers are going to say.'

'I think they'll be pleased,' Leandro said. 'In fact, I'm wondering if Jake's already guessed.'

She looked up him with a twinkling smile. 'You think?'

'I got a bit terse with him when he asked if I'd introduced you to any hot French or Italian guys.'

'Ah, yes, jealousy is always a clue.' Miranda gave a little laugh. 'Or so Jaz says. She'll be so thrilled for us. She's been itching to make me a wedding dress since we were kids. Now it's going to happen for real.'

Leandro brushed an imaginary hair away from her forehead. 'You will be the most beautiful bride. I can't wait to see you walk down the aisle towards me.'

'How long before we get married?'

'I'd do it tomorrow, but I think we shouldn't steal Julius's and Holly's thunder.'

Miranda loved how thoughtful he was. It was one of the reasons she loved him so much. 'I can wait a few months if you can.'

'It'll be worth the wait,' he said. 'We have the rest of our lives to be together.'

Miranda touched the side of his face with her hand, looking deep into his tender gaze. 'I don't care what life throws at us. I can handle it, especially if I've got you by my side. Which is kind of where you've always been, now that I think about it.'

Leandro smiled as he held her close, his head coming down to rest on top of her head. 'It's where I plan to stay.'

* * * * *

MILLS & BOON®
The Billionaires Collection!

This fabulous 6 book collection features stories from some of our talented writers. Feel the temperature rise with our ultra-sexy and powerful billionaires. Don't miss this great offer – buy the collection today to get two books free!

Order yours at
**www.millsandboon.co.uk
/billionaires**

MILLS & BOON®

Man of the Year

Our winning cover star will be revealed next month!

**Don't miss out on your copy
– order from millsandboon.co.uk**

Read more about Man of the Year 2016 at

www.millsandboon.co.uk/moty2016

**Have you been following our
Man of the Year 2016 campaign?**
🐦 **#MOTY2016**

MILLS & BOON®

Want to get more from Mills & Boon?

Here's what's available to you if you join the
exclusive **Mills & Boon eBook Club** today:

✦ *Convenience – choose your books each month*
✦ *Exclusive – receive your books a month before
  anywhere else*
✦ *Flexibility – change your subscription at any time*
✦ *Variety – gain access to eBook-only series*
✦ *Value – subscriptions from just £3.99 a month*

So visit **www.millsandboon.co.uk/esubs** today
to be a part of this exclusive eBook Club!